Contents

Other books by Terry Wroten

Natural Born Killaz

To Live & Die in LA

The Massacre

Girl, I Had Enough

Enough

NO BRAKES
PUBLISHING

A Novel

Los Angeles

Girl I Had Enough—Copyright © 2011 by Terry Wroten

Published in the United States by No Brakes Publishing
ISBN 978-0-9834573-0-5
PUBLISHER'S NOTE

www.wix.com/authortlw/nobrakespublishing

BOOKS ARE AVAILABLE AT QUANTITY DISCOUNTS. FOR MORE INFORMATION ABOUT BUYING BOOKS AT LARGE QUANTITY OR FOR ANY QUESTIONS ABOUT NO BRAKES PUBLISHING PLEASE WRITE TO NO BRAKES PUBLISHING AT NOBRAKESPUBLISHING@YAHOO.COM.

To contact the author, please write to authortlw@yahoo.com. You can also contact the author on both Facebook and Twitter at Author Terry Wroten

Printed in the United States of America

Book edited by Jill Alicea
Book cover designed by DaShawn Taylor
Interior Book Designed by Lishone' Bowsky

Dedicated to my mother
Mrs. Terrie Lynn Wroten
and my daughter
Terriyiah Lynn Wroten

To: Angie,

This My 3rd Book! Cant

Wait To Hear Your Feedback

Nice Meeting You! Love

The Support Once Again

Thanks Sis.

8-21-2014

CALVIN

1

Calvin, I ain't playin' with yo' ass. Nigga, you got two seconds to get yo' ass up or I'ma turn this house upside down!"

I leapt to my feet faster than a cadet at military boot camp. Alice was dangerous. She was as serious as AIDS in Africa and was no joke when it came to stirring up some shit. You talking about trouble maker! I learned years back when she burnt down our first house while I was asleep that she was no joke. I thought the girl was playing until my life was on the line and the smoke detectors started to go off like a five alarm fire. She kept threatening to burn the place down if I didn't get my black ass up to hear what she had to say. I took her threat as a bluff. I stayed asleep and death was lurking like a thief in the night. The house burnt down and by the grace of God, I made it out alive.

After all was said and done, I damn near killed Alice, but as soon as I gained enough strength to choke the bitch out, the police arrived. I had to literally walk around in circles over a hundred times crying. Yes, I said it! CRYING! I was crying like a bitch! So whoever said that men don't cry, that's a lie. I watched my house burn into ashes. All my family memories and all the hard-earned money I hustled on the streets to build the house was wasted. I couldn't believe I let a woman play me too close. It was like, *Damn, nigga, you just let a bitch fuck you out of a house and home.*

Terry Wroten

I was fighting my demons. I was trying my best to stay sane. Then, a voice roared in my head. It was my father, a man who took pride in raising my brothers, my sister, and me. A man who I respected dearly and tried my darndest to idolize. "My son, love your wife dearly, because every black woman needs a man to survive. However, if you got to put your hands on her, you don't need her and she don't need you! Like I've always told you and your brothers, a scorned woman is the most dangerous. Your best bet is to get the hell away from that girl before you end up in jail."

I walked to my car as my kids looked on and got my black ass out of Dodge. I went straight to my friends Byrd's house. Byrd was like a brother to me. We'd grown up together, and my father had actually paid his way through law school. He and his family accepted me into their home with open arms. I had another house I'd just bought on the Eastside, but I knew Alice was going to go straight there. I was in a no-win situation. I had plans on leaving her for good and getting a divorce. I stayed with Byrd and his family for six months. It would have been longer if Shalon, Byrd's wife, hadn't hooked me up with a friend of hers by the name of Lola Wright - Angel, as I called her.

After a few weeks of dating, I moved in with Angel. Angel stayed in the same gated community as Byrd, so it was all good. The gated community was two blocks away from the Inglewood Cemetery and not too far from the Great Western Forum. The location was great. Drama Queen couldn't just pop up announced. But after two years on the run from my family, I had to go back home. Byrd couldn't get the divorce to go through how we'd planned, so it was cheaper to keep her. Plus, I was missing my kids. But most importantly, they needed me, especially my fifteen-year-old son Calvin Jr. He was starting to hang out with the thugs on the block. He was missing school, claiming a gang, and was starting to get into trouble with the law.

When I told Lola the news that I had to go back home and that Byrd couldn't get the divorce to go through, she didn't protest. We'd become

12

Girl, I Had Enough!

a real close couple over the years, so I was expecting a fight. But to my surprise, she held fast.

"Calvin, I love you with all my heart. You showed and taught me a lot about myself that I didn't know even existed in me. Can't no one ever take that from me. You told me your situation from day one; I respect you for that. Wherever you are in this world, you will always be my man. These doors will always be open to you. I don't care if I'm dating or seeing someone else, which I doubt, the welcome sign will always be at the entrance."

Leaving Lola was one of the hardest things I ever had to do. It was hard because I couldn't stand Alice and was in love with Lola. Lola taught me the difference between a boss lady and a hoodrat: a boss lady knows her worth, and a hoodrat doesn't and will do any and everything short of death to find her worth. Lola also taught me how to love again. This is why I named her Angel. . . .

Anyhow, I leapt to my feet and Alice paced our room floor, in front of me, like a drill sergeant. "Muhfucka, I asked you, where was you last night?"

I let out a deep breath. I was getting tired of Alice and her shit. The day hadn't even started and she was stirring up some bullshit. "Come on, Alice, not right now. I'm tired."

I really was tired and not trying to argue with her. As one might know, it takes a lot of energy arguing with a woman; especially a ghettofied black woman! Drama Queen was ghetto with a capital "G". She didn't care how I felt. I could have dropped dead for all she cared. All she wanted was confrontation, and that was what she was going to get if I wanted it or not.

"Nigga, you think I care about you being tired?" she bellowed. "Nigga, me and the kids are tired our damn selves! Especially after stayin' up all night worryin' about yo' ass!"

The Kids!

The Kids!

Terry Wroten

The Kids!!!

This bitch brought the kids up every time we had an argument. I guess, it was her way of making me feel bad. The tactic worked on a regular basis, but I wasn't going for it this day. I snapped, "Bitch, our kids don't got nothing to do with this. You just want something to bitch about."

I felt an urge to just slap the shit out of her, but once again I thought of my father. "If you got to hit the woman, you don't need her, and she definitely don't need you. You gon' end up in jail, boy. I'm telling you. . ."

I waved Drama Queen off and walked into our walk-in closet. I slid on some jeans, grabbed my gun permit from my personal documents suitcase, and went up to the attic. The attic was where I kept all my guns. I had to relieve some stress, so instead of unloading all my frustrations out on the devil herself, I grabbed two hand guns and a sawed off shotgun and headed to the shooting range. As I exited the house, Drama Queen was at the door talking shit. Our white neighbors were just watching. They were used to hearing Alice rant and rave. I just ignored her, leapt into my Lincoln Navigator, and went about my business.

ALICE

2

I stood at the door cursing a storm. "Fuck you nigga! That's all you good for is runnin' like a bitch. That's why I wear the dick in this house, you pussy-ass nigga!" Calvin couldn't stand it when I strapped my dick on and went hard in the paint. He hated it. And I hated him— that was with a heated passion!

In the beginning it was all peaches and cream. I met Calvin at a Lakers versus Knicks game. Back in them days, the Great Western Forum was the place to be. Magic Johnson was the man. And the Lakers were doing their thang. I was nineteen about this time and a go-getter. I stand five-foot-nine. My skin color is cinnamon-brown with hazel eyes and jet-black wavy hair. I had a body of a Smooth magazine model and more curves than the projects I grew up in. I was born and raised in Watts, California, the Jordan Down Projects. I had two homegirls, Serena and Eve, who I hung with, went to school with, and did all my dirt with. We considered ourselves "The Get Money Bitches". We were all dimes in our own rights. Serena had secured season passes for us from one of her tricks, so this was one of our hustles. We'd hit the Forum and go straight to work. It was a fact that the Lakers attracted niggas with money to their games, and that's exactly what we wanted.

I ran into Calvin around third quarter. I left Serena and Eve in their seats. I just wanted to be by myself. I wanted all the attention and didn't need two other fine bitches with me. I knew I was going to run into some tricks, just didn't know I was going to run into a nigga I would eventually marry.

As I walked around the Forum I ran into a few cats who tried to holler, but I knew they weren't about shit. Then, I bumped into Calvin and two other niggas, who I'd later come to know as his brothers, Rasheed and Trey. Calvin grabbed my arm as I was strutting by. He spun me around and said, "Damn, ma, God must've sent you from heaven, because I was just praying to meet a girl like you."

I laughed at his game. It was weak, but not too weak, because he got me.

"What's so funny, girl?" he asked. "You think I'm playing? I'm serious. God must've sent you from heaven."

I looked Calvin in the eyes. They were mesmerizing. He wasn't a bad looking guy - actually he was my type, tall, dark, and handsome. His eyes were light brown. They complimented his Hershey Chocolate skin color and fitted him to a T. He didn't look like the kind of money holder I was looking for, but he didn't look broke either; especially not with the gold rope chain he had around his neck. I ended up exchanging numbers with him.

For our first date, I met him at Trey's house. Sheila, Trey's wife, forewarned me off top about Calvin. As soon as I knocked on her door and she invited me in, she said, "Girl, I'm not a hater, but I'ma tell you right now, you better keep it moving while you got a chance. These niggas are no good. I call 'em the Terrible Three. And the twins.... oh my Gawd! They sumthin' else."

The twins are Rasheed and Calvin. Trey is their older brother by three years. He was twenty-four. They were twenty-one and identical. The only difference between them is Calvin stands six-foot-one, and Rasheed is five-foot-ten.

I paid little to no mind to what Sheila was trying to tell me. To my nineteen-year-old frame, she just wanted something to talk about.

16

Girl, I Had Enough!

Calvin and I ended up catching a movie and dining out at a cool little restaurant. I was digging his style. Come to find out, his father was a crime boss—one of them old guys who hustled the streets his whole life and had money stacked up from the floor to the ceiling. But Calvin wasn't just living off his father. He and his brothers hustled. They were in the process of buying property and starting their own business. They were young entrepreneurs.

I fell in love with Calvin after our first date. Even though he wasn't as rich as the fish I was hoping to score while on the prowl with Serena and Eve, he had things going to achieve wealth. Plus, I was from the projects. He lived in Leimert Park. He was a breath of fresh air to me.

We had sex for the first time in a high rise suite at the Marriot down the street from the airport with the curtains open. It felt like the planes were so close passengers could see inside. This made the sex more exciting. I was loving everything about Calvin. I was in love. He said he was too. We were living just for the love of each other.

Two years after we'd gotten together, I conceived our first son, Calvin Jr. (CJ as everyone calls him). Calvin was proud. He overdid everything to express his appreciation to me for giving birth to his first child. He massaged my feet, ran my bath water, cooked and cleaned. We had a bond out of this world, one that I thought would never end; especially after he bought us a house and moved me out of the projects. Calvin spoiled me and our son so much, I was pregnant again within a year. Our second child was a precious little girl I named Joy from all the joy Calvin was bringing into my life.

After Joy was born, Calvin and I decided to wait a while before we planned any more kids. He was the best father the kids could ever ask for. Before I knew it, I was pregnant again. This time it was another boy. We ended up naming him Bill after Calvin's best friend Byrd's brother, Steel Bill, who got killed by some Bloods for wearing the wrong colors (but come to find out, Steel was a Crip, so the Bloods knew who they were after).

17

Terry Wroten

Calvin started acting weird after Bill was born. Even though my pregnancy, I felt he wasn't acting right. It was a vibe I felt. It wasn't that joyous vibe I felt through my first two pregnancies. It was something a woman feels when her man is cheating on her. Then, I got the phone call.

I was sitting in the kitchen watching Calvin wash CJ's hands in the sink. Bill was asleep in his crib. And Joy was running around the kitchen floor with a doll in her hand. The phone rang twice and I answered, "Hello!"

"Hello! Is this Calvin's wife?"

I arched my brows. It was a woman's voice on the other end of the phone. Calvin and I had gotten married after I'd given birth to Joy. The only women who called our house was my mother, Calvin's mother, his sister Sheila, who I'd become good friends with over the years, and Zena, Rasheed's new girlfriend at the time. Rasheed had a girlfriend every other week, so I wondered how long Zena was going to last?

"Yes, this is she. May I ask who's callin'?

"Well, this is Charlene. The woman your husband been sleeping with."

I damn near dropped the phone. I started to fume. I felt my project-ghetto-girl mentality coming on. I looked over to Calvin and shot him a murderous look. He asked "What?"

"Calvin, who is Charlene?"

His eyes widened. He was busted. His eyes told everything. His demeanor changed. He tried to snatch the phone, but I turned my back to him.

"So Charlene, how long have you and my husband been seeing each other?" I asked.

"Well, it will be a year next month. I'm calling because he lied to me and told me he was single when we met, but the other day when I told him I was pregnant . . . "

18

Girl, I Had Enough!

"PREGNANT!" I repeated disbelievingly.

"Yes. Two months pregnant!"

That was all I needed to hear. I couldn't take no more. I felt back-stabbed, betrayed, robbed, and violated. I felt less than a woman. How could Calvin do this to me? I put all into him. I mean, what was it? I wasn't enough woman for him? My pussy wasn't good enough? Where did I go wrong? I fell to my knees and cried.

Calvin picked up the phone and scolded Charlene. "Bitch, you fucked up! You didn't have to ruin my family. I told you to get an abortion, I'll pay for it. You didn't have to start all this shit!"

And that's just what Charlene did, start a lot of shit! The funny thing is, Calvin didn't even deny it. I knew niggas who got caught dead bang in the pussy and denied it. He didn't even say, "Let me explain" or nothing!

Calvin and I haven't been the same since. Our marriage had been on and off for the last fourteen years. 'Bout the time I became pregnant with our youngest daughters, the twins, I'd been with ten other men. Old habits die hard. As soon as we split and I went back to the projects, I was back hanging with my old crowd doing what we did best: get money!

After a year or two back in the projects, Calvin conned his way back into my life. This was when I conceived Alexia and Alexis, but things were never going to be the same. I was damaged goods with five kids and nothing to do. I planned on making Calvin's life a living hell. Misery loves company, and I was going to make him miserable as hell . . .

I cursed a storm as he left. "Yeah, Bitch Boy! Don't come back, because my nigga might be home."

Riiiiinnng!

Riiiiinnng!

As I cursed, the house phone started to ring. I slammed the door closed and ran to answer it. I was fuming. "Hello!"

Terry Wroten

As I cursed, the house phone started to ring. I slammed the door closed and ran to answer it. I was fuming. "Hello!"

It was Sheila. "Girl, what's wrong with you now? What Calvin do?" she asked.

"What he always do," I replied. "RUN!"

Sheila laughed. "Well, I was just calling to see if Rasheed over there, 'cause Zena been calling here all day looking for him. You know that girl gon' kill his ass one day. Watch."

"And I'ma do the same to mines . . ."

ZENA

3

Every time I got those bad feelings, I knew where they were coming from. I looked at my wedding picture. "Goddamnit! Rasheed, you just don't know what you put me through." I looked in my husband's eyes and cried. Thirteen years of pain, yet, love. I looked at my youthful face and wanted to put a bullet in my own head. How did I fall so foolishly in love? How did I fall for those sparkling eyes? And why I always fall for his charming ways?

I cried and talked to myself for hours. I knew Rasheed was being unfaithful. My woman's intuition was telling me that Rasheed was seeing more than three women. I mean, the clues were there. Coming home late, or not at all. Whispering on his cell phone in the bathroom, talking about it's business. And a major clue, he was tired all the goddamn time!

I was hurting inside. Rasheed had already cheated on me before with a stripper. And I took him back. I accepted his apologies and moved on. But just like the time I caught him cheating, my intuition was telling me. It was like I was trippin' and going crazy, but I wasn't. I even thought maybe I was insecure, but I wasn't. Everything I felt turned out to be true.

When I met Rasheed, I was eighteen and fresh out of high school. He was twenty-six. At first, I told myself he was too old for me, then I fell for him. He was a charmer. He showered me with gifts and the whole nine. To my young mind frame and way of thinking, he was a keeper. I gave in. I decided to give him a chance, and he took full advantage of it.

Rasheed swept me off my feet so decent, here I was looking at our wedding picture crying my heart out. Rasheed and I now had a two-year-old daughter, Maryam. I was scared to death to destroy my family, but if my husband couldn't keep his dick in his pants, I didn't need him. I told myself this over and over again, but deep down in my heart, I wasn't for sure what I was going to do if I found out Rah, short for Rasheed, was unfaithful. He denied it every time I asked him if he was cheating on me. I just needed to know the truth. I needed some closure in my life. I didn't know if I wanted to believe Rah or call Cheaters and hire an investigator. I was serious! Life was too short and I was aging fast trying to keep up with a cheater. I knew I was being stupid for sticking around, but I had found when I love, I love hard. Plus, Maryam needed Rah and me.

I sat the picture back in its place on top of the nightstand. I decided to go pick up my sister, Jada, so we could go shopping, and then she could take me to the nearest weed man. I only got high or drunk (well buzzed) when I was stressed. I wrote Rasheed a quick note letting him know my whereabouts just in case he made it home before me. He had Maryam with him for the day, so I knew he'd make it home this night. I grabbed my car keys and headed out the door.

RASHEED

4

I was at the house on the computer—Facebook.com— and watching my two-year-old daughter Maryam run around the room. I had just made it in from a long day out with Maryam. I decided to have a father and daughter day, because I was getting caught up with different business ventures and running the streets. I found Zena's note on the coffee table in the living room. It read:

I'm going shopping and might swing by Jada's house afterwards, so if you need anything call. Love Ya . . .Zena.

While Zena was out shopping, I had enough time to get online and chat with a few of my friends. I was addicted to Facebook like a crack addict addicted to crack, so I nickname it Crackbook.

Crackbook was my get-high and a way to escape reality. It was one of my dirty deeds, considering the fact that I was a married man with intent to meet other women to blog with, then eventually get in their panties. I set up my profile two years back with a picture of me rocking nothing but some boxers. My brother, Trey, and I hit the gym three to four times a week. My body was well-sculpted, even waxed, and marketable. I went by the name DickGameProper. After my first browse session, I learned how to navigate the site. I became Crackbook king. I started to live a double life as soon as I got my first email from a female called NaughtyGirl69. It read:

Damn, boo, you got body. (LOL) Where you at?

I laughed to myself. "Damn, technology make getting some ass ten times easier from when I was coming up." I replied to NaughtyGirl69 with a smiley face wink. She immediately replied:

Hi, sweetie, I'm not even 'bout to lie, I want to just touch your body to see if it's real. I'm a married woman, so no strings attached.

"Wow! Baby means business," I smiled, nodding my head. "But, damn, what if this is a set up?" I knew Zena's sister Jada stayed on Crackbook 24/7. She was the one who hipped me to the online network-ing site. I figured if she had a page, Zena had one too. I immediately went to NaughtyGirl69's home page. I hit the jackpot. NaughtyGirl69 wasn't my wife or any of her relatives. Her name was Tiffany, and she was a 31-year-old redbone looking for a man to satisfy her desires. Her husband was slacking in bed. She lived in Rialto, California. She was a go.

Tiffany was my first sexual encounter with a woman off of Crack-book, and she was not the last. Since her, I'd laced over fifty desperate-ly-seeking NaughtyGirls with the same come on. I courted women on the daily. Crackbook became my drug of choice. Every chance I got, I took a hit.

Maryam was behind me with a doll in her hand, running around the room in circles like a chicken with her head cut off. She was in her own world playing with dolls. I was in my own world navigating Crackbook to get some panties. This was until two things happened. First, I got an instant message from Jada. Somehow after two whole years, she found my page and busted me. Her message read:

I'm tellin' unless you pay me to keep my mouth shut . . .

Before I could respond to Jada's message, my cell phone rang. I fig-ured it to be her money-hungry-ass. I answered "What?"

Girl, I Had Enough!

However, it wasn't Jada. It was my mother. Momma was known to call at odd times. She wasn't too pleased with the way I answered my phone, but that was not the issue at hand. Poppa was sick. Old age was catching up to him. He had suffered a heart attack. He was at Kaiser. I immediately rushed to his side. He was the best father any man or child could ever asked for. I was there within no time . . .

ZENA

5

When I made it home from shopping, I found Rah's parking stall in our two-car garage empty, meaning he still hadn't showed up. It was getting late. I started hoping nothing bad had happened. Then, I started thinking maybe Rah was laid up with one of his flings with our daughter at his side. My mind started playing tricks on me. Where could this nigga be at eleven o'clock in the night with our daughter? I wonder what's gon' be his excuse this time?

As soon as I leapt from my car to start unloading, my cell phone went off. I looked at the caller ID. It was Jada. She had been calling every five minutes on the hour. I didn't make it to her house like I planned, because I got caught up in the grocery store. I was a shopaholic. Time crept up on me so fast, I decided to come straight home. I knew Jada was calling to curse a storm about me not showing up, so I decided to call her from the house phone once I got settled in.

"Zena!" Jennifer, the next door neighbor, called from behind her screen door. "Is that you?" she asked.

I hated stupid questions. "Bitch, don't it look like me?" I mumbled to myself. I took a dislike to Jennifer many years back. She was a young white girl in her late twenties who I just knew Rasheed was fucking on the side. But leave it up to him, they never fucked, they were friends. Well, they were too friendly for my taste!

Terry Wroten

I looked at Jennifer as she approached and forced a smile. "Hey, Jenn, what's up?" I wanted to go ghetto on her, but I couldn't. I wasn't raised in the ghetto. I grew up in a predominantly white neighborhood in Malibu, California. I wanted to say "Cracker bitch, what do you want?" but chose the norm. "What's up?"

"Oh, nothing much." Jennifer was happy-go-lucky. I wanted the bitch to at least act mean one time, so I could have bopped her in the mouth. BAM! "Bitch, that's for sleeping with my husband." And . . . BAM! "That's for being white!" I wasn't a racist, but I hated interracial dating. I felt black were supposed to be with black, and white supposed to be with white. So I hated the thought of knowing there was a possibility my husband probably slept with this cracker bitch.

I smiled. "So what brings you over here?"

Jennifer stuttered. "I-I got Maryam in my house."

I furrowed my brows. What in the hell was my daughter doing at this woman's house?

"Well, I-I don't know how to tell you this, but Rah-Rah's father is in the hospital."

My eyes widened. Poppa couldn't have been in the hospital. I'd just called him before I started stressing over my marriage. Shit, honestly, he and Momma was the reason I started to stress. After hanging up with them and sensing the joyous mood they stayed in around each other, I started thinking over my marriage, and I wondered if Rasheed and I would last up to 45 years like his parents?

Jennifer continued, "Rah told me to tell you he suffered a heart attack a few hours ago and to call him when you get in. But do you want me to go get Maryam? Or do you want me to watch her?"

I didn't know how to answer that, but I knew one thing for sure: I didn't want this bitch to get the satisfaction of fucking my husband and watching our daughter. I was going to call Rah, and if he wanted me to come to the hospital, I was going to take Maryam to her aunt's house.

Girl, I Had Enough!

But other than that, I hated hospitals. I lost both my parents in a hospital, and after damn near killing Rah after he cheated on me with that goddamn stripper, hospitals brought back bad memories.

Maryam ended up coming home. After I got all the groceries out of the car, I called Rah. I looked over at the nightstand, and the red light on the answering machine was blinking. The digital numbers under the message light read: 11.

"I know they all from Jada," I told myself out loud. "Damn, I know I stood this bitch up, but why in the hell is she blowin' my phone up like this? Something must be wrong."

CALVIN

6

Yeah, meet me up there. I'll be waiting on ya'll."
"All right, in a few."
I called Byrd and Rasheed as soon as I got in my truck and drove off.
They decided to meet me at the shooting range. They knew that I had
got into it with Drama Queen before I even told 'em. It was no secret
that I ran to the range every time I got into it with the wife. Unlike most
men, I didn't drink, so the shooting range was my bar. But eventually,
dealing with Alice, I will follow the trend.

I made it to the range an hour before Byrd and Rasheed. I had emptied over ten clips before they arrived. Each target practice I thought
of Drama Queen and emptied clip after clip, aiming at the head. Bull's
eyes! If this was reality, she would have needed a closed casket funeral.
It was a shame how much I hated my wife and the mother of my five
beautiful children but I couldn't help it. I made one mistake thirteen
years back, and she just wouldn't let it go. It was like every time she
saw my son, Charles, by Charlene, or even thought about him, she made
my life a living hell. However, two wrongs don't make a right, so I
never brought up all the trifling deeds she committed when she thought
I didn't know she was fucking every nigga in the projects. I even took
her back after some cat called Joe showed me a porno with her in it getting gang-fucked by four cats who all looked grimy. However, through

all this I took her back, yet I was still the bad guy.

As I thought of all the bullshit I was putting up with dealing with Alice, I shot. I mean, all the mental and emotional stress and the childish games she played … in my head, this was my get back. I wanted the bitch dead.

Boom, boom, boom, boom, boom, boom, boom, boom, boom, boom!

"Bitch, die! Bitch, die!" I thought as the bullets ripped through the paper target. I repeatedly did this over and over until Byrd and Rasheed arrived with Maryam and Trey in tow.

"Damn, bro, you wish death upon someone, huh?" Byrd snickered.

"Yep. Sure do," Trey added, emerging from the snack area where Rasheed and Maryam were seating sharing ice cream. I didn't see them when they arrived, so I took it Trey was with Rah when I called him. But come to find out, Rah called Trey after we hung up. My twin didn't do nothing without Trey. It was as if they were the twins and I was the older brother.

We ended up in the snack area with Rah and Maryam. Maryam ran over to me. My niece was getting big. I hadn't seen her in a few months. She was Rah's only child, which was surprising. Out of everyone in the family, even our younger sister, Carrie, expected Rah to have at least ten kids by then. Rah went through women like they were sneakers. Also, surprisingly, he was still married to Zena. I'd lost thousands betting that he wouldn't make it past a year of marriage. I don't know how he did it, but whatever he was doing was working. Well, that was what I thought.

"Man, Zena been stressing a nigga out lately," he informed me as I held Maryam in my arms. "A nigga come home, and she want to smell a nigga's dick and the whole nine. I hollered at Poppa, and he told me that mean she's on to something. He told me whatever I'm doing, I need to slow down, but a nigga is addicted to Crackbook. I think I need to check into sex addicts anonymous or something of that nature."

I forewarned, "You better do something before she finds out or gets fed up with your shit. Remember what her crazy-ass did last time."

Girl, I Had Enough!

Rah laughed. "Look who's talking, and look where we at. We only come here, why? Because Alice probably was 'bout to pull another Left Eye on yo' ass."

The whole table doubled over in laughter except me. I didn't see nothing funny. My situation was no laughing matter. At times, I did laugh to myself about how my life had gone from all good to all bad. It was like laugh now, cry later. I felt like one of them Southwest commercials: I wanted to get away.

Just at that very thought, my phone started to ring. Perfect timing, I told myself. I was just hoping and praying it wasn't Drama Queen. I glanced at the caller ID and smiled. It was Angel. I answered on the second ring.

ANGEL

7

I had gotten off of work and was tired. I'd pulled a long twelve-hour shift at the hospital. I was supposed to stay longer, but I couldn't. I couldn't stop thinking of Calvin. I remembered him telling me the story about how his childhood friend Steel Bill got killed. Calvin was with him. They were at the wrong place at the wrong time, chasing pussy, as Calvin told it. A car drove up on them and started firing on them for no apparent reason. This was right off of Crenshaw and Jefferson Blvd. across the street from West Angeles Church. At the time, Bill and Calvin were just thirteen-year-old teens who had on the wrong colors, coming home from the movies with two teenage girls. The car rolled up on them and fired repeatedly sending an entourage of bullets into Steel's upper torso. He was hit twenty-nine times, and he died in Calvin's arm.

I cried, hopping in my Lexus leaving work. Steel's story played in my head every day. Kids were committing genocide against each other nonstop over two colors: Red and Blue. These two colors were destroying our kinsman, our race, our culture. It made my heart ache seeing so many young black men being rushed into the hospital. Most of them we couldn't save, because bullets had struck a main artery or there was just no way to survive.

I thought of this every night as I ran from one emergency room to the next. Then came the thought of why we black women outnumber black men twelve to one. I did the math. Every time another young black man dies from gang violence, another young black man enters the penal system. Then you have retaliation, so the drama and tragedy repeat itself. But what about the mothers and fathers whose cries fell on deaf ears, who wanted help but could not get it? What about the child they lost either to death or the system? Now they're faced with the reality of losing a beloved child or two. What they do? Turn to some form of substances. What about the sisters and daughters who got the ass end of the stick and had to deal with the aftermath, who have no parents and no brothers to love or show them the right way? What they do? Sort love and affection in the streets…look for love in all the wrong places, ending up with AIDS, HIV, or some kind of venereal disease.

These people entered the hospital every day, every hour, every night. And these people weren't just people, they were young black people, the people who were supposed to carry the torch after my generation exited. But it was like they were dying and killing each other so fast, there wasn't going to be no generation after me.

The hospital was taking its toll on me, but I refused to give up. If I gave up, that was one less life I could have saved. On this night specially, EMT rushed a thirteen-year-old into ER. He was seconds away from death. His friend held his hand crying "Nate, please, don't die on me. Man, I love you." The boy's whole body was filled with his friend's blood, but 'bout the time I rushed over, death had taken his friend's life like a thief in the night.

The boy fell to his knees and started screaming, "Why!" I felt a sense of urgency to go comfort the young man. I held him in my arms and cried with him. I felt his pain. He and his friend were just two innocent kids coming home from football practice when a car rolled up and started firing on a crowd of gangbangers, but bullets do not have names. Two of them struck his friend. Both bullets hit main arteries.

Girl, I Had Enough!

"We were just coming home from football practice," he sobbed. "And they started shooting."

I sobbed with the boy until his parents showed up. My pager was going off nonstop, but I couldn't just leave the boy. He reminded me so much of Calvin; my will wouldn't let me leave. I held the boy as tightly as I could. Wholeheartedly, I knew he would never be the same. I felt for him. I felt for Calvin. I had to see him to let him know I cared. It was hard to explain what I was going through, so I just grabbed my purse out of my locker and clocked out.

As I left work, I found myself crying the whole ride home. When I made it home, I ran straight to the toilet. I had to vomit. This was something I hadn't done since med school. Back then, I stayed with my face buried in the bowl, witnessing such horror and tragedy. Over the years, I would somehow become immune to dreadful and unfortunate happenings. But this calamitous event was too close to home and ripping at my heart.

After I threw up my lunch and dinner, I decided to hop in the shower and straighten myself up. I needed to see Calvin, but I knew he didn't like how I stressed myself over my work. He'd told me on many occasions that he respected my occupation, but I was too beautiful to be working in ER. He told me I had a way with words and was a powerful woman who needed to be a motivational speaker, instead of an emergency-room physician. I had to pull myself together before seeing him.

After I got out of the shower, I slid on some jeans, a matching halter top, and some tennis shoes. I wrapped my hair with a scarf and decided to head to Krispy Kreme. I had a sweet tooth and loved their donuts. Plus, the nearest one was in the old neighborhood Calvin had grown up in, so I knew he wouldn't have a problem meeting me there—unless his wife was somewhere around.

Terry Wroten

I hopped back in my Lexus and headed for my destination. I was smiling from ear to ear knowing I was going to see the man I desperately loved. But was I wrong for loving the next woman's man? Or was I human? I actually didn't know myself, but I knew one thing was for sure, I was always told to follow my heart. And that's exactly what I did. I followed my heart.

ALICE

8

Riiiiinnng!
Riiiiinnng!

I was just about to bleach Calvin's clothes when the phone started ringing. He had me boiling like a tea pot. First, he ran like a bitch in the middle of an argument because he stayed out all night. And he probably was with that stuck-up-ass doctor bitch. Whoever he was with, I didn't know, but when I confronted him about it, he copped an attitude and left. What was that stupid-ass comment he'd made? Oh! A good run is better than a bad stand any day. I wanted to slap the shit out of him for saying some bullshit like that to me. However, that was his point of view, and he stuck to it. Every time we got into it, he would poof and disappear. I was tired of his shit. I was planning on doing some shit to have him think before he just got up and left. I'd already taught him one lesson when I burnt down our house. Now, I was going to teach him another.

I ran to the phone, thinking it was Sheila ready to spill the news that she busted Trey cheating or that Zena had finally killed Rah. Rah was playing with fire when it came to Zena. That girl was a card or two short of a full deck. I mean, I probably acted crazy and did some trifling shit but I didn't have the guts to walk around with a gun in my purse trying to catch my husband,cheating. To me, it wasn't that serious. It was more like you do you, and I do me. We both could play the cheater's game.

I answered the phone on the third ring. "Hello!"

"What's up, ho'? What you doin'?"

It was my girl Serena. "Shit, nothing much. 'Bout to bleach this nigga's clothes and then set his truck on fire while he's asleep."

"Oh shit! What he do now?"

"What he always do. Run!"

Serena chuckled. "Well, bitch, I was just calling to tell you somebody got out, but who?"

"Who? You know half the projects is locked up."

"Girl, that nigga Tyson!"

"Ooh! You lyin'."

"Sheeeit! He got out this morning."

Tyson was a nigga I used to mess with when we were fourteen. He was the first to get between my legs. We were real close at one point in time, but he couldn't seem to stay out of jail.

I asked, "Girl, how he look?" curious to know if he was still fine.

"Bitch, that nigga lookin' good. He don't even look our age. He look about twenty-five. And the nigga on swoll. Nigga look like Tyrese or somebody. Tall, dark, and sexy."

"So who he fuckin'? I know one of y'all stank bitches took my man down."

"Yo' man, Serena repeated. "Ooh! But naw, he did ask me about you when I saw him a few minutes ago. He gave me his number to give to you."

"Okay. But you still ain't answer my question. Who the nigga fuckin'? I know bitches are fighting over that dick."

Serena agreed. "And you know they are. Bitches like sharks when fresh meat hit the water. But Tyson say he ain't fucking with nothin' right now. So you better try to get it while it's fresh.

Serena hit it right on the nose. I had a new plan. "Girl, you damn right I'ma get it while it's fresh. What's the number?"

Girl, I Had Enough!

After I got Tyson's number from Serena, we hung up. I looked at Tyson's number with the phone still in my hand. I dialed it. As the phone rang, I thought of one of Trina's songs and started popping my ass while looking over my shoulders. "Pull over that ass too fat. Whoot. Whoot!"

"Who dis?" Tyson answered on the third ring. He still had that sexy thugged-out voice of his.

I smiled. "Boy, yo' momma didn't teach you to answer a phone like that," I taunted.

He smiled. I heard it in his voice. "Oh shit! This is my girl, Alice."

"Sure is. I see you still remember my voice."

"Shit, how could I forget it? All the many hours we spent on the phone talking nasty."

I laughed. "Hush."

"Anyway. What it do, ma? What da muhfuckin bidness is? You still married or what? You know a nigga dick been drier than the Mojave Desert for the last ten years, so what it do?"

I laughed again. Tyson was known to keep it gangsta. He spoke his mind and was a beast in the bedroom. I liked it rough. I like it hard. And I liked when a man spoke nasty to me. My sex life had gotten boring with Calvin. I knew I needed some of Tyson's good loving and sexual healing, and to add icing on the cake, I was going to get it in the bed Calvin and I shared. There was no shame in my game. He played dirty. I played dirtier. I was a devious bitch from the beginning to the end. I didn't have nothing to hide. I told myself I was going to fuck the shit out of Tyson, and if the dick was still good, I was going to move him in. A bold move, huh? Yep. Sure was! Matter of fact, I decided to call Calvin after I settled scores with Tyson. Calvin was going to learn his wife was a cold bitch and thathe fucked up cheating on me.

CALVIN

9

"Hello!" I answered my phone, stepping away from my brother, who was still laughing at Rah's corny-ass joke. Maryam was still cradled in my arms.

"Hey, boo, are you busy?" Angel asked on the other end of the phone.

I was smiling like the cat who ate the canary. "Yes. I'm right here with my brother and Byrd. But give me a few minutes, I'll call you right back."

"Okay."

I hung up with Angel, looked over at the boys, and in unison they said, "That must be Ms. Lola Wright."

I smiled. "Ya damn right. I'm outta here."

I kissed Maryam on the forehead and sat her in her father's lap. I grabbed my guns, returned the eyes and ears I borrowed from the range, and left the three stooges sitting at the table cracking jokes on me.

I called Angel as I entered my truck. She answered on the first ring as if she was just waiting for me to call her right back. "Hello!"

"I see you couldn't wait 'til I called back. Or was you 'bout to call bachelor number two?"

She giggled. "You starting to figure me out real well, aren't chu?"

I laughed. "Yeah, I guess so."

Terry Wroten

"Calvin, Negro, don't play with me. You know, Ms. Lola Wright is all yours."

I joked, "How could I tell?"

"Mr. Williams, if you know what's best for you, please don't play with me."

"Okay. Where are you?"

"I'm in the neighborhood you grew up in. I'm right off Crenshaw and Vernon. I'm headed to Krispy Kreme. You feel like meeting me there?"

I agreed. We hung up. Krispy Kreme right off of Crenshaw and King was only twenty minutes away from the shooting range. I got there in ten. I parked my truck right next to Angel's Lexus and approached the entrance of the famous doughnut shop. As soon as I walked in, two young hustlers draped in black with backpacks around their chest shouted "CDs! DVDs!"

"Get 'em while they hot!"

I admired the two young men. They were hustling bootleg material, but it wasn't crack or drugs. I had to give it to the two young entrepreneurs, they were starting off better than my brothers and me. When we decided to become hustlers, we went straight for the easy money. I liked what I saw in the young hustlers; they were doing something positive.

I ended up buying three CDs from the two teens. I only planned on buying one to support their cause, but they had game about themselves. After I bought Smokey Robinson's greatest hits, they knew what type of music I was interested in.

"Oh so you's a 70's slash 80's type of music man, huh?" one of the two asked me.

I nodded.

"Well, check this out, if you add another five dollars to that ten, I'll add this Earth, Wind, and Fire Greatest Hits. Man, this joint right here got major hits on it, such as "Devotions", "Tonight", "September" and many more. You know what I'm sayin'?" Yo, this the shit right here."

44

Girl, I Had Enough!

I couldn't deny the young hustlers. They were slicker than snake skin. They had the gift of gab. And I just knew they were some young players, because they got me to buy the third CD by saying, "And since we know that beautiful lady seated at that table over there is here for you, give us five more dollars and you can take this Anita Baker home with you. You know this is a baby-making CD, right here, so you will be guaranteed some good stuff with this."

I wanted to ask the young hustlers what they know about getting some good stuff, but I just bought the three CDs and walked over to the table Angel was seated at.

"It looks like you guys were having a decent conversation," Angel said as I sat next to her.

I smiled "Yeah. Kids these days sho' can trip you out. These kids are ten times more advanced than our generation."

Angel nodded in agreement. "Yeah, with this new technology, I believe each generation will be more advanced than the other. But all in all history repeats itself. I catch myself doing things my parents did back in their day. Now I see why that saying 'been there, done that' makes so much sense."

I agreed. Angel continued on about different topics we face in every day life. Angel could have been an activist. She was a powerful woman. She just didn't know how powerful she was. She touched on topics most Africans didn't talk about, like how we are the main cause of our rapidly decreasing numbers in our population. She said, "We can't blame the white man no more. We got a black man running for president. In the 60's and 70's, I can understand. But today there's no excuse."

I nodded nonchalantly. Angel was up on all current events, especially the ones that were affecting black communities throughout America, such as gangs, drugs, AIDS, etc. She talked about AIDS like she was a spokesperson for AIDS awareness, but I got the hint.

"Lola, if you trying to say I should get tested, baby, please just say that. I know you already think I'm fuckin' every Mary, Sherry, and

45

Terry Wroten

Berry in town, but no, sweetheart, I stopped chasing pussy years ago. Like I told you, my best friend got killed from us chasing the cat."

Angel felt apologetic, but why should she? With all the crazy stuff going on in America, I couldn't trust Alice for nothing in the world. No telling who she had been sleeping with on the side. Or during the two years I was gone.

I trailed Angel to her house after we chit-chatted over coffee and doughnuts. We took Crenshaw all the way to Manchester, then Manchester all the way to her gated community. During the drive, Alice was blowing my cell phone up. I ignored Drama Queen, because I knew all she wanted to do was make my life miserable and start some shit. I couldn't see how she could just spend all her time and energy trying to destroy me. I gave the woman everything. Neither she nor the kids needed or wanted for anything. But I guess two different characters with different beliefs would collide all the time. She was loud and wild. I was humble and at ease. She was ghetto and drama. I was silent and laid back. We fell in love with each other when we were young and on the same page, but with time comes change and more change. I changed for the better. She changed for the worse. I put up with her for the kids. But my patience was running thin. She was playing with fire and didn't know it.

I ended up answering because Drama Queen wasn't going to let up until I answered. And two things I didn't want to do was turn my phone off, just in case of an emergency, and I didn't want my phone to be ringing nonstop in Angel's presence.

I answered, "What?"

"Damn, nigga, you don't got to answer your phone like that! I was just calling to let you know I hate you . . ."

"I know that! And?"

"Well, since you know that, I also want to tell you since you walked out on me and the kids, don't come back home tonight because I got one of my friends over here."

Girl, I Had Enough!

I could've broke that bitch's jaw for playing me so close, but I knew Alice; those were the type of games she played. I shined her on. "Well, have a good night and a good time, because I sure will," I taunted.

I hung up.

Angel's place was the same way I had left it when I went back home. She didn't change nothing, not even the way I positioned the flat screen TV on the wall, which she hated 'cause I had it opposite of the couches. She once protested, "Why in the hell do we have couches if you got the TV where we can't see it if we're sitting on them?"

My response: "Shit, we don't need 'em. We don't have company anyway."

I positioned the TV on the wall so I could watch football from the garage. There were multiple televisions in the garage, but none came close to the 62-inch plasma. As I looked around the house, my cell phone started ringing. It was Drama Queen again! I didn't answer.

Angel looked at me and shook her head. "Mrs. Ghettofied, huh?"

I nodded.

Angel frowned "What she want?"

I replied "Drama."

She chuckled. "Hummph."

I said, "Yep. She'll learn one day."

"Well, why don't you just answer and tell her you are busy?"

"Because I just did that on the way here."

"And what she say?"

This was just what I didn't want to happen. Now I had to explain to Angel, but she understood. She knew my situation. "Well, she called to say she hated me and don't come home 'cause she got one of her friends over. You know, I didn't intend on going home anyway, so her drama tactic didn't work. I got you."

I kissed Angel on the forehead. She looked at me with her sexy innocent-wide eyes and said, "Calvin, I love you. Can't no one take that from me."

Terry Wroten

Angel's words opened me up. She was teaching me how to love again.

Just as I was about to tell her I love her, my phone rang. At first, I was going to pay it no mind. Alice was getting on my nerves. I picked it up without looking at the caller ID.

"What! Whatta fuck you want?"

"Gosh! Boy, I don't know where you and your brother learned how to answer y'all phones, cause I sho' ain't teach y'all such rude manners."

Oh shit! It was Momma. I immediately apologized.

"I know, you don't got to tell me. I know you and Rasheed is having marital problems. Or should I say girl problems? But I know one thing, if you don't wanna be snuff, don't snuff nobody. Playing with a woman's heart is like playing Russian roulette with your life. Anyhow, I'm calling because your father just had a heart attack. I'm at the hospital . . . "

That was all I needed to hear. I was out the door headed for the hospital with Lola right on my heels.

RASHEED

10

Poppa lay in his hospital bed sedated when I arrived at the hospital. He had gone off medicine I'd never heard of and could barely pronounce. One I did recall was called Nitro, some drug that kept the heart going or something like that. Shit, this was what Lola had told me when she and Calvin had arrived. I didn't know nothing about medicine, so I was glad Calvin had Lola at his side. I asked her everything I could think of. Why they got that oxygen mask on him? Is he going to make it? What do you think triggered him to have a heart attack? Why this? Why that?

I asked the dumbest questions. I was in a state of panic. I panicked so much, I had to go wait outside and smoke a cigarette. I hadn't smoked a cigarette in twenty years. But it was what I needed to calm my nerves and clear my head. I was acting worse than Calvin and Momma. Poppa had figured me to be the stronghold of the family.

My younger sister, Carrie, arrived at the hospital after I had smoked my fourth cigarette and was headed to the elevator to smoke my fifth. Carrie was the standout and star of the family. She was an actress and had scored roles in big budget movies. My sister was doing good for herself. She and the actress Meagan Good look identical. They could have played each other's double.

Carrie asked, "How is he?"

Terry Wroten

I shook my head and massaged my temple with a Newport between my fingers. "I don't know. Shit, ask Lola, Calvin girlfriend. She's a doctor."

Carrie looked me dead in the eyes. "Rasheed, you are not taking this too well, huh?"

I nodded. "Never envisioned our old man in a hospital like this. Go see him . . ." I paused. I felt tears roll out of my eyes. I did not like the thought of losing my father. It was heartrending. "Go see him. He look all fucked up."

Carrie was a strong woman. A strong black woman! She fought her way through Hollywood. She fought her way through an all-white college. I should have known she was going to be the strong one out of the bunch. "Rasheed, Poppa is getting old. He has lived a long life for a man of his caliber. You should have known that the clock was going to start ticking sooner rather than later. So don't go given up hope and turning back to old habits, because you know they die hard."

Carrie pointed at the cigarette in my hand and walked off. "Poppa said you'll be the stronghold, not the weakling, so pull yourself together, Rasheed," she said over her shoulders.

I stood outside the hospital pacing the sidewalk back and forth for the fifth time. This was my fifth cigarette. My mind was speeding. I didn't know what to do. I didn't know what to think. All I wanted was for Poppa to pull through. Just as I thought that to myself, my phone rang. It was Zena. I forgot to call her on my way to the hospital. Truthfully I didn't want to call her. I didn't know if Jada had called her and told her about my Crackbook page or not? I didn't want to hear her mouth either way it went, so I took Maryam over to our neighbor's house, and told her to watch Maryam 'til Zena pulled up.

"Hello!" I answered not knowing what to expect, but I didn't care. My father was in the hospital and probably wasn't going to make it. I wished Zena would have said something about Crackbook; I would have whipped her verbally with so many B-words it would have been

Girl, I Had Enough!

a shame. But as they say "she knew what was best for her".

"Hey, baby, I just got the news. Is everything all right? Want me to come down there? How is he?"

I didn't know how to respond. Shit, I didn't know if I was all right, so I sure couldn't say how Poppa was doing. All I knew was that my father had had an heart attack and it was life-threatening. However, I said, "Right now, I don't know how he doing. But, naw, I don't need you to come down here. I'm all right. I'll call you if I need anything."

I hung up with Zena and lit another cigarette. "Boy, life is getting hard on a nigga."

ZENA

11

After I hung up with Rasheed, for some odd reason, I just felt he was lying. Then I told myself it wasn't nothing but my insecurities. That was one thing I knew fa sho', Rah wouldn't lie about his father being in a hospital. He loved Poppa too much to be using his name in vain. I just wondered why in the hell he didn't want me there by his side? Not like I wanted to be there anyway, but I did feel an urge to be at my husband's side.

I put the groceries up and put Maryam to sleep. I was about to hop in the shower when my phone rang. I knew it was Jada for the umpteenth time. I decided to prolong my shower to answer the phone. I sensed what my sister had to say was going to stir up some emotions. I answered, "Hello!"

"Damn, girl, I've been calling you for the last two hours. Where the hell you been? And yo' ass stood me up."

I lied. "Girl, I didn't even go shopping. Rah's father in the hospital. He had a heart attack."

Jada held her breath. "You lyin'. Is he all right?"

"Rah don't know right now, but he said he'll call me as soon as he find out."

Jada sighed. "Well, I was calling to let you know what I found out today on his ass. But since his father is in the hospital, I'll wait."

Terry Wroten

My blood pressure shot sky high. I knew my sister had some valuable information I needed on Rah. She was part of my investigation team that I put together to spy on his ass. I had called Cheaters and filled out the paperwork to have some Cheaters investigators on detail, but they never got back at me, so I had to work with what I had. And Jada was my all-star player. She was the Miss Info of the hood and the family. No! That's an understatement. She was the information hotline for everyone in Los Angeles County. For a little bit of change, she was known to get the dirty on anyone. Jada worked for the DMV, so it wasn't hard for her to find out what was what and who was who. What was that motto she used to have? Oh! 'We only want the skinny when reading the newspaper. We want the thick 24/7 here.' I knew Jada had some reliable info, and I wasn't about to let it pass.

"Jada, you already know not to play with me. You already know how I feel about my husband, but if you got something, you need to tell me."

"Zena, I got something I want you to check out, but I want you to promise me you won't say nothing, at least until his father's situation is over."

"I promise."

I made that promise not 100% sure what my younger sister was about to tell me, so honestly I wasn't sure how I was going to act. As much as I felt my mind was playing tricks on me, I knew I was sitting on a powder keg.

"Zena, listen, I know this is not much, but I was on Facebook and I found out that Rasheed got a page on there. Something told me to go to browse and see all the people in a five mile radius of me. I immediately spotted Rah…"

I didn't know too much about Facebook, but I knew it was the new trend for young and old. I cut Jada off. "So what you find? We can skip all the unnecessary stuff. Just tell me what you found."

"Well, look, I'm just going to give you his page address so you can go check it out. But while you at it, I want you to go to this other nigga's

Girl, I Had Enough!

page and tell me what you think about him. I met him at work. He'd just gotten his driver's license and was so happy . . ."

Jada was known to jump from one subject to the next without blinking an eye. My sister was a true gossip queen. She would have talked all day and all night if I would've let her. I cut her off. "J, I'm not tryna hear who you ran into at work or who finally got their driver's license."

"Shit, if you want Rah's Facebook page address, you'll hear me out. Because I want you to check out my new little friend's page and tell me what you think. Girl, he's fine as hell too."

"Okay, Jada, just hurry up and tell me, 'cause now you got me wondering what the hell Rasheed got on his page?"

"You'll find out as soon as I finish telling you about my friend I met today. Well, his name is Darrell. I know that because I did all his paperwork. But he go by TLW. He's an author . ."

"TLW!" I repeated, cutting Jada off again. I was reading one of his books called *Position Of Power.* And I had another called *Ghetto Love* that I was going to read next. I was halfway done with *Position Of Power*, and so far I couldn't put the book down. It was a page turner. If it wasn't for my marital problems, I would have finished the book in one sit-down. But, all in all, I was a fan of TLW's work. My friend Twila had given me the two books to read. We were in the same book club, and no one had ever heard of TLW until she bought him up. And just like she had told everyone, he was a good writer. I had to admit it, he was.

Jada responded "Yes. T-L-W. Why, have you heard of him?'

I smiled, feeling like I knew a star. "Yep. I'm reading one of his books right now, and it's good."

"What's the name?" Jada asked. "Because he signed and gave me his first two books, *Killa Black* and *The Gangsta & The Gentleman.* I read both of them. Now I just ordered *Drama From The Baby Momma* and *Position Of Power."*

Terry Wroten

I chimed in. "Well, I'm reading *Position Of Power.* And I got *Ghetto Love* in the cut."

Jada and I talked about TLW like we were groupies. Come to find out Jada had met him at work. He had just passed the driving test. She was the instructor and test giver. After he passed, he kissed her on the cheek. He was so happy to have his driver's license. He told her his whole life story about how he was only twenty-two, and had just re-entered society after being gone since age fourteen, and was trying to get his life together. He told her that receiving his driver's license was one of his biggest accomplishments other than getting his GED and writing several books. He went in his trunk, handed her two books, signed them, and gave her his Facebook hook-up.

I felt somewhat happy for TLW. He was trying to do something with his life after pulling so many years. I mean, most brothers got out of prison with no goals or skills to achieve anything. Like my younger brother Jake, who was Jada's twin. He was twenty-eight, had been in and out of prison since age fifteen, and seemed like every time he got out, he was worse than when he went in. I was elated for TLW. Plus, his work was good. I liked him.

"Anyway. Here's Rah's and TLW's page addresses. Let me know what you think about him?"

I got both web pages and hung up. I wanted to see how TLW looked, but his page had to wait. I walked over to the house computer, forgetting all about the shower, and went straight to Rasheed's Facebook page. I couldn't believe my eyes. The first thing I saw was his display name, 'DickGameProper. I kind of laughed to myself, but I was hotter than fish grease. I told myself, he going to learn about playing with my heart.

RASHEED

12

I was outside the hospital smoking cigarette after cigarette after cigarette, like a choo-choo train when my brother Trey and his wife Serena, pulled up. Word had spread like a wildfire, and folks were filing into the hospital left and right to check on Poppa. I didn't realize how powerful of a man my father was until everyone from their mother to great-grandmother started showing up. My phone was ringing off the hook with people calling me to confirm if Poppa was really in the hospital. One person was Alice. I don't know how she found out, but when I answered my phone, she was on the other end asking, "Is it true Poppa in the hospital?'

I didn't know what to tell her. I knew even though she hated Calvin, she loved Poppa. How could she not? The man literally came to bat for her all the time. He'd bought her cars, clothes, and paid the tab on the house she burnt down to keep her from going to jail after she acted like she didn't care. He treated her like she was a biological daughter. He didn't care what she and Calvin went through, she was still his daughter and mother of five of his grandchildren.

Poppa actually believed Calvin turned a good girl bad. He told Calvin that he brought her wrath and treachery on himself. He ended up telling me the same thing after Zena put me in a coma for two weeks. She clubbed me over the head with a gin bottle that put me right out

Terry Wroten

after catching me cheating with Deanna. Deanna was a stripper I met at Trey's strip joint, who turned out to be more than a pole dancer.

However, I told Alice to call Calvin. I wasn't getting my nose caught up where it wasn't supposed to be. I didn't want to tell her yes, knowing she would pop up, and that Calvin had Lola with him. I planned on telling him as soon as I finished my cigarette and journeyed back into the hospital.

Trey leapt from his white Mercedes Benz CLS with dark tinted windows and chrome 22-inch rims, looking like a million bucks. My brother was a smooth cat and carried himself like an old school gangsta/pimp, but he was neither. He even owned a few strip clubs, but he didn't consider that pimping. Trey stood an inch or two taller than me. Even though he was Poppa's junior, he resembled Momma. His skin color was copper-brown. He had long hair that he kept pressed, like Katt Williams. He was slim-built and stayed dressed to impress.

I chuckled to myself as Trey leapt from his car, brushed the non-existant wrinkles from his shark-skin slacks, sucked his teeth, and strolled my way with Sheila in tow. She was draped in the latest Rodeo Drive fashion. You just knew they were well-off.

"How's he holding up?" Trey asked as he walked up, extending his hand.

I slapped him five and puffed on my cigarette. I casually turned opposite of him and blew the smoke out. "Shit, I wouldn't be able to tell you," I informed. "But when I was up there, he wasn't looking too good, with tubes all down his throat and shit. Man, this shit is all bad."

I felt the flood gates give. Tears rolled down my cheek in rivers. I was going through it. There I was, a 39-year-old man weeping in front of a hospital. People must've thought I'd lost a loved one. Trey wrapped his arms around me and hugged me tight. It was one of them consoling big brothers' hugs. Trey knew how close Poppa and I were. Growing up, my family was a close-knit family, but everyone had their favorite sibling or parent. Trey and Momma were one of a kind. They had a

58

Girl, I Had Enough!

mother-and-son bond that was out of this world. Calvin and Carrie were so close, we called them C and C. And I was considered Poppa's mini-me. There was no secret that I was his favorite child.

Trey held me tight. "He gon' be all right just have faith," he assured me, releasing his grip and backpedaling. "Poppa is a survivor. Like he used to tell us when we were younger, he's a soul survivor. He said, 'if I was to die today, I will still be alive. I'm a soul survivor. I live through my kids'."

Trey was no doubt my big brother. He knew how to restore a little faith back into me, because I was straight giving up. I just knew Poppa wasn't going to make it. He looked too weak. The heart attack had him looking like someone had strangled him with a plastic bag wrinkling his face. I mean, how could a dark-as-midnight man get so red?

"Carrie and Momma called me with the news. I was at the club getting some shit situated, but nigga, you hold strong."

I nodded, taking another deep pull off the cigarette. Just as I was about to say, "I'm all right," Alice walked up with a big swoll cat, who I could tell was fresh out of prison. We nodded "wassup" respectfully to one another, but didn't exchange any words. Alice stopped right in front of me with her hands on her hips. I could tell from the look on her face she was about to say something outlandish.

"You know, you and your twin are two pains in the ass. You coulda told me Poppa was in the hospital."

I screwed up my face. I was really starting to see why Calvin hated her. She was not as confrontational and ghetto when they first met and got together. Well, lets just say, she didn't show it. I actually liked her back then, and even encouraged Calvin that she was a keeper. But over the years she changed, and not for the better. It seemed like the older we got, the more immature she got.

I shook my head. I felt that Calvin was her husband, not me! I snapped, "Look, Alice, if you don't getta fuck out my face…"

Terry Wroten

Before I could finish my sentence, Trey jumped between us. He knew she had to be stupid to step to me while my father in the hospital.

"Come on, Alice, you, your friend, and Sheila go on upstairs. Rah and I will be up there in a minute."

The threesome disappeared into the hospital. Trey glanced back at me. "Nigga, back to what I was saying. Nigga, you hold strong and don't fall back on them thangs." He pointed at my Newport. "You know they hard to kick."

I nodded. "Yeah, I'll be all right."

Trey patted me on the back. "Yeah I know you going to be all right. I'm just scared you might let this situation do you in, so later on, why don't you stop by the club? I might have a little something to cheer you up."

He playfully nudged me in the side with his elbow. I smiled. "As much as I would love to take that offer, you know I can't. Remember what happened the last time I messed around at one of your clubs. My black ass was carried out on a stretcher."

"Yeah, that's 'cause like Poppa always tell us, you play with fire, you get burnt; that's some true shit. But if you take fire and put it next to something that's fireproof or resistant, you can't get burnt. It's like you gotta make calculated steps. Cat Daddy, you just can't go in the rain forest without a raincoat. It's shit like that that gets niggas caught. That's why Calvin's situation is so fucked up, and why Poppa says y'all ruined y'all wives."

Trey was going into one of his pimp modes. He was known to try to spit game at Calvin and me. Half the time the game he spat was real, but the other half was out of his own league. He probably was big brother and all looked good on the outside for him, but he was having marital problems too. It was like, come on, nigga, you going through the same shit as us, but tryna spit some shit to us that ain't even working for you.

I listened to Trey spit his so-called game while I finished my cigarette. After I flicked it, we went to check on Poppa. As we got off the

Girl, I Had Enough!

elevator onto the floor Poppa was being held on, Alice and Calvin were in the nook of the hallway face to face. The dude who came with Alice was standing not too far off with his hands in his pocket, watching Alice's every move. She was moving her head from side to side like she was telling Calvin off. Calvin's facial expression said the same thing. Trey and I looked at each other and smiled. Drama Queen loved to stir up some shit.

I found Lola at the nurse's desk talking to the nurse. She was also eyeing Alice and Calvin, but wasn't trying to make it obvious. I pulled her to the side. "So what are they saying?" Lola, the eternal optimist, smiled. "Cheer up. Y'all father going to be all right. His tests just came back. He got heart disease. I read his records, and they show he has been having heart problems for years now."

I furrowed my brows. Lola had to be wrong. I had never seen or heard Poppa complain or talk about having heart problems. However, she was a doctor. I knew as soon as Poppa got well, I was going to ask him about this. Poppa and I were close, so I wondered if he knew about this heart problem, or if it was something new to him too?

I continued listening to Lola. "Y'all father is getting old. He can't be doing things he used to do when he was younger. But, all in all, he will live to see another day."

That was all I needed to hear. I bear-hugged Lola for the information. I didn't care about all the drama Alice was stirring up in the hospital. My father was going to live another day. I was relieved. I felt good. It was time to call it a night.

TREY

13

I dropped Sheila off at home and kissed her good night. "All right, baby, I'll be home after I close the club."

Sheila nodded "okay" and walked into the house. We'd been out all day. We started the morning at the Beverly Center. Sheila loves to shop. I could have lived without it, but I had promised to take her shopping as a make-up present. I'd been out and neglecting my wife. It wasn't that I didn't love her, because I did. I was just caught up in a web of trying to support our expensive living habits and keeping up with all the young tenders I had on the side. Plus, I was paying my daughter's college tuition and trying to help my son start our own record company. My hands were full, and the one person that was feeling neglected was Sheila.

I met Sheila back in college. This was before I dropped out, deciding to be a full time hustler. I was a petty hustler in college. I sold pot here and there to all the white boys and pot-heads around campus. Then some of my boys I grew up with started moving weight from state to state for Poppa. This was 1984, the beginning of the crack era. My boys were making so much money, they couldn't hide the fact that they were working for my father from me. One spring break I came home and found my boy Ray in my house stashing some cocaine in the attic. No one was home, so I became furious. I rushed Ray to the ground and started punching him in the face.

He started yelling, "Trey, be cool! Be Cool! Poppa got me doin' sumthin'."

Come to find out, Poppa had Ray moving kilos of cocaine for him, and Ray was in the house because Poppa gave him the key. Poppa thought he was slick. He had taken the family out shopping while Ray filled the attic with dope. And the funny thing is, he was using dudes I grew up with and thought I wasn't going to find out.

"Trey, I'm telling you, don't tell Poppa I told you anything. He made it clear to the whole crew that you are not to know."

That spring break I kept my mouth shut and went back to school, but I wasn't focused like my first semester. I started partying like a rock star. I didn't care. I had a career at home. My grades started to plummet. Eventually, I was called into the dean's office, put on school probation, and had to sign up for tutoring.

My first day of tutoring, I found out my tutor was a junior named Sheila Brown. I was a freshman, so I didn't know too many people yet. But my boy Sam Baker told me Sheila Brown was one of the finest sisters at the school, but didn't mess with dudes. Sam thought she was a lesbian.

"I'm telling you, bruh," he said, "she's s fine sista, but either she's munching on pussy or just don't like brothas. Every brotha in this school done tried to get at her. She don't even give a Negro a 'Hi" or 'Bye'. Watch, you gon' see."

I was sitting in the library when Sheila walked in. I knew who she was as soon as she entered. The girl was an African Goddess, just like everyone had told me. She stood five feet tall, cinnamon-brown skin, wide chestnut eyes, head full of silky black hair, and she was voluptuous with perfectly round breasts. She was eye candy. I started licking my lips.

She spotted me sitting at the designated spot and forced a smile. She walked over and introduced herself with her hand extended. "Hi! I'm

Girl, I Had Enough!

Sheila Brown. I'm your tutor."

I took her hand and brought it to my lips. I gently kissed the back of it. "Nice to meet you. And nice to have such a beautiful woman as my tutor…this might encourage me to do some work."

Sheila snatched her hand away from me with the quickness. She looked at it like I had violated her. I immediately apologized. "You know, if I caused any harm by my actions, I apologize."

She twisted her lips. "Say sorry."

I screwed my face. "Girl, you must be crazy. I already apologized. I'm not no sorry Negro, so I'll never say I'm sorry, but what are you? Some kind of lesbian or something?"

Sheila smiled. "Take your seat over there, boy." She pointed opposite from where I was already seated. I was in her seat.

"Don't call me boy. I'm all man."

"Boy, you ain't no man. What make you a man?"

I simply replied, "'Cause I am."

Sheila smacked her lips. "Anyway. Boy, let's get to work."

"You gon' learn about calling me a boy, Girl."

Sheila took her seat after I moved to mine. She asked, "What I'm going to learn, Boy?"

I was starting to like our little standoff of words. I sensed I was opening Sheila up, so I went for the kill. "You gon' learn what they say about calling a man a boy."

She rolled her eyes. "What they say?"

"Uh, I rather not say. I don't want to hurt your feelings like I did earlier."

"Don't bite your tongue now," she challenged.

I smiled. "Well, they say you take a boy, you suck his dick, you turn him into a man."

That was the beginning of something new. Within two weeks of tutoring, Sheila and I were a couple. She couldn't deny my wit if her life depended on it. Before the end of the school year, Sheila was pregnant. Sam Baker and a few of my other college buddies came to me slapping me five.

"Man, you did it," Sam Baker said. "So guess she's not lesbian after all."

I slapped him five. "I guess not."

I lasted one year in college. When I returned home, I told Poppa that Sheila was pregnant and that I want to join his team. I told him I knew everything he was doing, so he couldn't deny me. That summer, I traveled the USA more than the president. I felt I didn't need school. I was a made man.

It was a quarter to twelve after I'd dropped Sheila off at home. She wanted to ride to the club with me, but she had to get up for work in the morning. I was glad. I hated having her around my place of business. I did things I didn't need her to have any knowledge of.

I arrived at my place of business, Red Light District (RLD), a little after twelve. It was a Friday night and crowded. RLD was my third strip club. I entered through the back door. Fat Pat, my head bouncer, followed me up a flight of stairs to my office. He gave me the run down on all that had taken place throughout the day. Nothing exciting, so I waved him off at the entrance of the office.

He nodded. "Well, I'm 'bout to get back to work. If you need anything, just holla."

Fat Pat was an ex-lineman for the Chicago Bears before he blew a knee. I looked him dead in the eyes. "Big Guy, you know if I need anything, your big ass will be the first I call."

He smiled. We exchanged pounds. And he headed back downstairs. I opened the door to my office and shook my head. My office was built like a mini condo, equipped with a 32-inch plasma TV, two Italian leather couches, a built-in bar and kitchen, and a desk with all the office necessities. However, on the couch, KC, Sheila's sister and co-owner of the club, was receiving oral sex from Candy. They were going at it. KC was a complete lesbian, and she was manlier than me. Candy was one

Girl, I Had Enough!

of our newest and youngest dancers.

Seeing them go at it was not a surprise to me. This was the way KC and I recruited. Believe it or not, after KC was done with Candy, Candy was going to bring more young tenders around to make money and get their freak on. KC and I were good at this. Red Light District was making money right out the gate with this plan. And I planned on fucking Candy.

I stepped into the office and had to squeeze my legs together, trying my best not to rise like yeast. KC and Candy were two beautiful girls. They were dimes and had the bodies of some goddesses. I couldn't help but grab on myself once to stop my Johnson from expanding.

KC chuckled as she saw me do so. "What's up bruh-bruh?" she asked in a deep voice—a voice that did not match her beauty and bangin' body.

I sighed. "Nothing much. Just gettin' in to relieve you of your shift so you could stop blowing up my phone."

KC leapt up from the couch, pussy fat and hairless. I was immediately turned on. If she swung my way just a little bit, I would have committed adultery, which was something I did very often.

"So how's Poppa?" she asked, sliding into her pants. "And it look like someone like what he see. Can't resist temptation, huh?"

She nodded at the bulge in my slacks.

I chuckled. "Natural instincts, that's all."

"Yeah. I know that's right." She looked at Candy and told her to get back to work. I glanced at Candy's backside as she exited the office and knew I was going to have her come right back up after KC left.

After Candy left, KC and I went over business. All was well, so she disappeared without further ado. I walked over to the bar and poured me a shot of Jack Daniels. I couldn't stop thinking about how fat KC's pussy looked. It looked tight, warm, and juicy. I found myself grabbing my crotch and squeezing down on my dick. I wanted to fuck KC bad! Just the thought of knowing dick had penetrated her in years turned me on and had me hard as steel. However, she was my wife's sister, that was never going to happen. My next best bet was Candy.

I walked over to my desk with the shot of fiery liquor in my hand. I took a seat, went over some papers, then looked at the monitors stacked on the desk. I had cameras all around the club. I saw everything that was going on from the office. I spotted Diamond on the pole. She was one of the oldest dancers we had. She'd been around for years. And even though she was rounding the corner of her early forties, she still had it good. I'd stuck my dick in her more than a few times. She was what I called my shortstop. When I got horny and wanted just a quickie, I stopped by Diamond's house.

I looked over to see who was working the bar and spotted Ayana mixing drinks with nothing on but a G-string. She had a nice set of breasts: perfectly round, perfect mahogany-brown circles and nipples. And a perfectly beautiful face to match. One thing KC and I did was keep LA's finest in our club.

I looked over to Fat Pat's post at the door. He was talking to some young pimpish-looking cat. RLD was located right off of Hawthorne Blvd. and Century, which was considered a ho' stroll. Pimps had their stables working Century like it was Sunset or Figueroa. With the race track and airport on Century, the ho' stroll was a big money boulevard. With this knowledge, they figured that they could come into RLD and gorilla pimp on our girls. Fat Pat and the rest of his team of bouncers were known for pouncing on pimps and throwing them out of the club.

As I looked at the monitors, I saw the pimp wave Pat off and turn on his heels. I grabbed the mic to the PA system and called Fat Pat to the office. He looked into the camera positioned at the entrance of the club and gave me thumbs up. A few minutes later he was at the office door. I buzzed him in.

"What up boss?" he asked, huffing and puffing like he had just run a five-mile marathon.

Girl, I Had Enough!

"Boy, you all right?" I replied, looking at him. "You want some drank or something?"

Pat was known to make himself at home; that was one of the reasons I kept his big ass out of my office. "Shit, hell yeah, let me get a few shots of that Jack." With Pat, nothing was one or two. It was always a few. But I understood. He was feeding like three or four people. I told him to take the whole bottle.

"Anyway. What was all that about at the door?" I asked as I downed the fiery liquor I had poured myself a few minutes earlier. I made a funny face and wiped my lips with the back of my hand. That initial shot was always too strong for me.

Pat replied, "Man, that young pimp nigga, Moon, always comin' in here on some bullshit, so I told him tonight he gots to bounce. That kid think I'm playin' with his ass."

I laughed. "Don't hurt him, Tyson. Anyway, what's the low down on Candy? Have you tampered with the pussy yet? I think her young ass is ready."

Pat shook his head and smiled. He started rubbing his palms together like he had hit the jackpot. "Man, I don't know about the pussy, but the head game is magnificent. I had that a couple of nights ago, but the young broad wouldn't give up the pussy."

"I wouldn't want yo' big ass on top of me either." I laughed. "I need you to call her up here and don't let nobody bother us. Know what I mean?"

Pat nodded. "Got you, boss. But, man, don't hold me up all night, because I got Ayana's ass lined up for the night."

I chuckled and slapped Pat five. We were some fools when it came to the women working at the club. And the funny thing is, we compared notes just like the women did in the dressing room. Some nights, I just sat up and listened to the whores, and they were all some crafty bitches. And best believe everyone was fucking everyone, someway, somehow.

69

SHEILA

14

"Oh yeah! Fuck this pussy, girl. Fuck it!"
KC was on top of me pounding away. Her 10-inch strap-on was doing wonders. I loved how she gyrated her hips with each penetration. KC was a woman, so she knew how to please me. I locked my legs around her waist and back to match her thrusts. I moaned at the top of my lungs as she dug deeper inside me, sending chills up my spine. I'd been sleeping with KC for years. We knew each other's bodies like the back of our hands. I loved her as much as she loved me.

We started dating back in college. This was before I met Trey and had told myself I'd never mess with another man again. Men were cruel. They didn't care about the women they said they loved. If they did, why did they hurt us? I felt this way after two previous relationships I had. I'd found when I love, I love hard. I loved each man I'd been with wholeheartedly, only to get burnt. Not once, but twice! I finally decided that men are nothing but liars, cheaters, deceivers, and heartbreakers. It was in their nature to do women wrong. After two failed relationships where I came out the victim, I was fed up with men in general. They couldn't do nothing for me, but live life and die.

I met KC my freshman year of college. She was a sophomore on the girl's basketball team. She was good. So good that if the WNBA was in existence, she would have went pro. KC stood five-foot-nine—tall for a woman who had more curves than Buffie the Body. Her skin color was butterscotch, and her head was full of wavy hair. She looked mixed. I figured she was Puerto Rican and black, but I was wrong. She turned out to be all black, just with a good gain of hair.

We spotted each other on campus one day and immediately connected like magnets. It was like we knew each other and knew we both swung the other way. Over the years, I would eventually find this to be true: a woman that's gay or bi-sexual will know off top that the next woman is gay or has bi-sexual tendencies.

"I see you checking me out," KC said bluntly as we bumped into each other. I couldn't deny it. She was a comely woman, and I had already explored my sexuality with two different girls. It was on from there.

'Bout the time I met Trey, KC and I had been seeing each other on the low for a year and a half already. All the brothers around campus tried to holler during this time period. There were a few handsome ones like Sam Baker and I forgot the other guy's name, but men were not for me. This was until Trey's smooth-talking ass signed up for tutoring.

When I walked into the library, I immediately shook my head. I'd seen Trey around campus a few times. He was known as a party animal. I also heard he was selling a little pot. I didn't know him from Adam or Eve, but attending a college like UCLA, the handful of blacks either knew each other or knew of each other.

Our first tutoring session didn't go too well. Somehow Trey's slick-talking ass got me out of character. He kissed the back of my hand and said, "It's a pleasure meeting you." I pretended to not like his approach, but I had to give it to him, he was sharp—sharper than a needle. Then, he had the nerve to say, "You take a boy, you suck his dick, you turn him into a man."

After two weeks of resisting temptation and sticking to my script, I couldn't hold strong any longer. I fell weak. Trey's suave game was too much for me and he swept me off of my feet. Plus, Trey was attractive,

Girl, I Had Enough!

well-proportioned, and very imposing in appearance. I opened my heart and legs to him and have been with him ever since.

I introduced KC to him as my sister. And it has been like that for twenty-four years. Trey never had a clue that we weren't family related, but sexually related. The only thing he knew was I had a lesbian sister who was his business partner and sister-in-law.

As KC dug deeper and deeper into my womb with her strap-on, sending me to la-la land and beyond, I laughed to myself. Payback was a mutha. Trey thought I didn't know nothing about all the bitches he was sleeping with at the club. I'd been with him too long not to know his every move, but I played along with it. Like I said earlier, I know all men are dogs, and that while he was at the club he was doing what he did best: CHEAT! KC came over and fulfilled my burning desires. As long as Trey was paying the bills and filling his duties as father to the kids, this could have gone on forever.

KC made me climax more times than I could count. She then buried her face between my legs and massaged my clit with her tongue while her fingers danced around my womb. Sounds of pleasure filled the room. I moaned nonstop.

"Oh! Yes! Yes! Yes!"

"Eat this pussy, girl!"

"I love it!"

"Oh! Oh!"

"I'm cummin'!"

"Yes. Right there!"

"I'm cummin'!"

Every time KC buried her face between my legs, my pussy rejoiced. I was a 45-year-old woman, but felt twenty-five. My sex drive was at its best. I was having the best of both worlds. I wasn't planning on stopping no time soon. My situation could not have been any better. I tried to tell Zena and Alice that the twins were just like their older brother. I told them, especially Zena, that there was no reason to be sitting up crying

Terry Wroten

all day over two no good mutherfuckers, because the more good they did for the twins, the more bad they got in return. It was like, you do good, you get treated bad. You do bad, you get treated good . . .

TREY

15

Candy walked back into the office wearing a topless costume and some stilettos. Her perky breasts stood at attention. Her full lips were covered with gloss. She had a flat stomach and pierced belly button. Her pussy was so fat, her thong barely covered the giant. Her strut was of a runway model. She had her hair pinned up in a bun. I looked her dead in the eyes. She knew exactly what I wanted. I told myself, I'm 'bout to tear this pussy up. Candy was fresh, only eighteen - a young tender.

I licked my bottom lip. "How good is it?"

"Mines the best, baby."

I smiled. "Is that right?"

"Yep."

"Well, what's the ticket?"

She curled her lips. "Since you my boss, just slide me a buck and a half, and we'll call it a date."

I dug into my pocket and produced what she wanted. I sat the money on my desk and got undressed. Candy slid out of her costume and asked, "How do you want it?"

I chuckled. Out of all the dancers I'd exchanged sexual favors with over the years, not one of them had ever specially asked me how I wanted it. I replied, "Let's make this fun. How do you want to give it to me?"

Terry Wroten

Candy curled her lips again. "Well, if I give it to you like I want to, you'll be sprung like T-Pain." She started mimicking T-Pain's single, "I'm sprung . . ."

I laughed. "After all these years in the bidness, you get a nigga like me sprung, you gots to have some platinum pussy. That virgin-tight shit."

"Well, that's what it is, boo-boo."

Without another word, Candy grabbed me by the shaft of my dick and led me to the couch. I took a seat. She turned her backside to me like she was about to give me a lap dance. I slid on a condom. She spread her legs and bent slowly and carefully onto my dick. When the opening of her womb touched my dick, she let out a low moan. "Whoooooooool!"

Her pussy was fat yet small. She couldn't just slide down onto my shaft. She had to gradually work her way down. To my surprise, her pussy was virgin-tight. It was like trying to fit an elephant into a dog house. She slightly bounced up and down on the head of my dick until her pussy allowed me access. Once in, Candy sucked in air as her pussy adjusted to the length and width of my pipe. Her womb clung onto my boy like a boa constrictor. It was squeezing the life out of me. It was warm, wet, and tight. It was definitely the best I'd ever had.

As Candy gradually picked up the pace, I realized she knew how to work her inner muscles. Every time she bounced up and down her womb gripped tighter onto my boy. She was moaning and sucking air through her clenched teeth. Her pussy was rejoicing. It made swishing noises as our bodies connected.

Within two minutes, Candy was vehemently slamming herself up and down on my dick. She was holding her ankles and popping her pussy. "Fuck this pussy, nigga."

"Fuck it!"

"Whool Yeah just like that."

"Don't stop."

"Just like that!"

Girl, I Had Enough!

Her head was between her legs. The only thing I saw was ass and pussy. I became excited. Over-excited! Her pussy was so tight, the condom broke. It was so good I didn't pull out, and within seconds I exploded inside her. That was the quickest I'd ever nutted. I felt like a one-minute man.

Candy chuckled after she leapt up from my lap. "I told you, I got the fiyyah. I got that 'dro." She walked over to the desk, grabbed her money, slid back into her costume, and went back to work.

I told myself "Damn, that was some fiyyah!"

I knew I was going to return for seconds and maybe thirds, I just had to play my cards right. I didn't need KC to find out and tell Sheila, so I had to make sure Candy kept her mouth shut. I called my partner in crime: Fat Pat. He was good at carrying out my dirty work.

ALICE

<u>16</u>

3 Months Later

Y ou like that?" Tyson asked in a teasing manner.
I didn't reply. I was at the peak of a climax. I didn't want the
feeling to go away. He removed his head from between my legs and
inserted his big dick. He held my legs over my shoulders and started
gyrating his hips in a circular motion. He proceeded to pound away.
He had at my pussy like a pit-bull mixed with a jackrabbit with no
emotions. He was fucking me so good that tears rolled freely from out
of my eyes. He had stamina and was at me like a madman, like I had
stolen something from him. He was stroking me in a way only a nigga
fresh out of jail knew how. Underneath me, a lake was forming from
my juices. I loved it rough. I loved it when a nigga just put it down. It
brought out the wild side in me.

I moaned. "That's right. Fuck this pussy, baby. Fuck it like a porn
star."

"Show me that you still can put it down."

"Oh shit! You hittin' the spot. Yeah, nigga, hit that shit. Hit that shit.
And you bet not stop."

I wrapped my legs around the small of his back and met his thrust. I
started fucking him back.

"Whool-wee! Fuck this pussy, daddy."

"I love it."

Terry Wroten

"I'm cummin'!"

"I'm cummin'!"

"Don't stop!"

I didn't want Tyson to stop. He was putting it down. I nutted so many times, I couldn't keep count. I was dripping like water. Tyson fucked me until I went numb. I caught paralysis. I even felt when he nutted inside me. He rolled off of me onto his back. He was lying on Calvin's side of the bed looking at the ceiling like a dead cockroach.

When he caught his breath, he asked, "Now what?"

I furrowed my brows and looked him in the eyes. "What you mean 'now what'?" I was confused.

"Alice, man, we been fuckin' for the last three months now. Your kids don't like me, especially your son. That li'l nigga moved with yo' busta-ass husband's folks. Yo' husband act like he ain't trippin', but I'm hood nigga, I know he is. And you talkin' about you pregnant. We gotta do something."

Tyson was right. I cupped his chin. "Baby, don't worry. I'ma make it right. I promise."

I was sprung. The way Tyson worked my middle was like no other. I didn't want to lose him. We had history. Plus, I was thirty-seven with five kids and one on the way, and the last three months, things had been real heated between Calvin and me. I put him out! He moved back with that doctor bitch. He filed for divorce again. I filed for child support. He called me a bitch. I called him a bitch nigga. He hated my dude. I hated his bitch. We were at war. And like Tyson said, we had to do something. The only question was, what was the best thing to do?

CALVIN

17

Only intense conflict, turmoil and pain can explain why I was sitting outside my house with a .50 Cal Desert Eagle in my hand plotting to kill Alice. She done pulled the last straw one too many times. I gave her chance after chance. I couldn't take it no more. I sat in my car drinking some Easy Jesus (E&J). I didn't usually drink, but the bitch drove me to tipping the bottle. She was the core of all my problems. She was deliberately trying to destroy me. And the crazy thing was, she looked me dead in the eyes and told me, "A scorned woman is the worst enemy to have. I'ma make your life a living hell."

She kept her word.

I leapt from my car, pistol dangling at the side, and jogged to my front door with a Sean John hoodie on. I planned on dumping her body in the LA River. I wasn't thinking about the consequences. I felt like Mary J. Blige: "I wasn't gon' cry and I needed no more drama". All Alice stood for was drama. I knew after all was said and done, I was going to be the black Scott Peterson, because Alice was three months pregnant. By who? Not me! The only kids I cared for was the ones already here. The unborn had to be her boyfriend's, because it sho' in the hell wasn't mine. The last time we had sex was five months back. The timing didn't add up.

Terry Wroten

Just as I opened the door to enter the house to catch Drama Queen and her boyfriend fucking in my bed, a car pulled into the driveway. I frowned. "Lucky bitch!"

It was Alice's mom and my children. I about-faced out of the house and met them at the car. My three daughters rushed me. I was glad my pistol was holstered, because I wasn't expecting them to be jumping all over me, especially after all the bullshit Alice had put in their heads.

"Y'all father ain't shit", and ,"Fuck him! He don't do shit for y'all! He don't love y'all! He left y'all for that doctor bitch!"

Drama Queen made me out to be the bad guy. But in reality, I was the one who took care of everything and everyone. Ms. Ghettofied never worked a day of her life. She wouldn't have been able to tell you what a work check looks like if her life depend on it. Now, a welfare check, that was a different story. But, all in all, she told the kids that "daddy wasn't shit." Truth be told, "Momma wasn't shit!"

However, I did not feel comfortable with putting the children in our mess, so I never disputed anything Drama Queen told them. The only child of ours I told was CJ. He was old enough to know the real. I felt, why have the kids going through our struggles? At least wait until they got old enough to understand and pick whose side they want to be on. And that was exactly what I did with CJ. And the funny thing is, 'bout time I sat him down and told him the honest truth about me and his mother, he already knew.

"Daddy, where you been?" Joy asked, hopping onto my back. She was a big girl, fifteen and a half. My knees almost buckled when all her weight came down on me. Her left leg tapped the butt of my gun. By the grace of God, it stayed in the holster. I told Joy to get down.

"And to answer your question, I been busy trying to make sure y'all taken care of."

Joy put her hands on her hips. "So busy that you don't come check on us? Remember, you promised, you'd never stay gone over three days without seeing us."

Girl, I Had Enough!

That was painful. I thought back to the day I promised my daughters that. It was after I disappeared on them for two years. I felt like I was letting them down. I didn't know what to say. This was the stressful part of not being at home. How could you tell a child, daddy's not home because I don't get along with your mother? It could have been done, but I was brought up that adult business is adult business, and a child stays in a child's place. What kind of parent would I have been spilling their mother's dirty laundry to them? Alice did it, and thought it was hurting me, but it was only hurting the kids.

As I thought of something to say to Joy, she pulled my shoulder down, so she could whisper in my ear. "Daddy, I know you lying. You ain't been around 'cause Momma got a new boyfriend. And we hate him. You see CJ went to live with Granny and Poppa."

I did not like lying to my daughter. I felt awkward. It was like stabbing myself in the heart. Joy was at the age where I could have sat her down and told her the goings on between her mother and me. However, right then and there was not the time. Alexia and Alexis were standing right next to her. They were only twelve.

I decided to change the subject. "I promise, I'm going to make everything right. Just give me some time. Anyway, where's Bill?"

Bill was my fourteen-year-old son, whom I named after my best friend, Steel Bill. Honestly, he was the last child I had with Alice that I felt was mine. I loved the twins, but something in my heart kept telling me they weren't mine. Around the time Drama Queen conceived the twins, we were having problems. Our marriage was rapidly going down hill. She was seeing other people, and I was doing the same. It was like, you do you, and I do me.

"Bill stayed over at the house," Alice's mom informed me. "He wanted to hang out with his grandfather a little longer."

I nodded, thinking about how Alice was just like her mother. Mrs. Jones knew I was a good man and father, but she wouldn't dare tell me to my face. She was a churchgoing woman who thought she was holierthan-thou, but she was the devil in disguise. Alice got all her character flaws from Mrs. Jones. It was like that saying, "she get it from her momma".

Just as I thought of the she-devil, she emerged out of the house. She screwed her face up seeing me. "What the hell you doin' here?'

I held fast. "To see my kids . . .And, if I recall correctly, I believe I bought this house with my hard-earned money."

"Well, it's mine now . . ."

"Oh shit! Here comes trouble," I mumbled to myself before Drama Queen could finish her sentence.

"When you walked out of this house for the umpteenth time and final time on me and your kids, this house became solely mines."

I wanted to say, "Yeah right! Bitch, that house, apartment, unit, or whatever you want to call that slum you left in the projects, is solely yours." However, I decided on a more humble approach. "Alice, don't start getting beside yourself in front of the kids, all right? We both know whose hard work, sweat, blood and tears got us this house. So let's not go there, all right?"

I went back to talking to my daughters. Drama Queen hated it. She snapped, "Joy, you and your sisters get y'all asses in the house!"

Joy tried to protest. "But Ma . . ."

"But Ma, nothing! Get in the house! I told y'all Calvin-ass don't care about y'all!"

I started to fume. I was letting Alice get under my skin for the umpteenth time. Joy looked at me as if to say "Daddy, please, say something . . ." Once again, Alice was playing her trump card, the kids. She put them right in the middle of our bullshit. I couldn't play Mr. Nice Guy no more.

I snapped. "Look, lady!" I yelled. "All I want to do is spend time with my kids. You can take your ass back in the house with all that craziness."

Girl, I Had Enough!

Just as I finished my sentence, her boyfriend walked out of the house with his shirt off. Ex-con was written all over him. He looked like Damien (Terry Crew) from the movie Next Friday.

"Ay homey, if my girl say bounce, then kick rocks."

I shook my head and laughed. This fool didn't know what he was getting himself into. He was literally putting his life on the line for a piece of pussy. I laughed out loud "HA! HA!"

"What's so funny? Cuzz, you didn't like what I said or something?"

He started walking my way. I said a quick prayer. "God, please, don't let this man walk up on me in front of my kids and my property." I then warned him. "Bruh, please, don't step to me in front of my kids. Alice will get you caught up in some shit. I'm warning you, my man, don't take another step towards me."

Captain Save-a-Hoe kept coming. He looked like Incredible Hulk or some buff action figure. I stepped in front of my daughters and drew heat. "Muthafucka, I said don't disrespect me in front of my kids!"

This fool walked into a death trap. If it wasn't for Joy, he wouldn't have lived another day. My daughter came from behind me and jumped in between us. I heard her say, "Daddy no!" But it was too late. I'd already fired twice. Luckily something told me to shoot upward, because I would have killed my own daughter. Both bullets hit the top of my house.

I looked at my kids, then at Damien. They were all shaking like dice in Vegas. I glanced at Damien and told him to get ghost. He ran out of the yard and up the block with the quickness. I knew he would eventually come back with his boys, so I decided to make my departure before any harm came my daughters' way. I kissed Joy on the forehead and apologized. "Baby, I'm sorry. I didn't mean for things to turn out the way they did. I'ma make this up to you. Plus, you old enough to understand my situation with your mother, so I want to talk to you one-on-one. Okay?"

Joy nodded, wide-eyed. I just knew I had scared the shit out of her. I kissed her again on the forehead and went into my pocket. I handed her and the twins a crisp hundred dollar bill each. I then kissed them the same way I had kissed Joy, and told them I love 'em. I walked to my car.

Behind me, Alice taunted, "Yeah, you better leave, nigga! 'Cause yo' bitch-ass going to jail. You no good muthafucka!"

I ignored Alice and drove off. I laughed all the way to Angel's house. My situation was no laughing matter, but I had to do something before I went crazy. I laughed and sipped Easy Jesus all the way there.

ALICE

18

No that muthafucka didn't!" I told myself out loud, pacing my living room floor back and forth. I was contemplating calling if I should 911 or not? In the projects, we were programmed to never dial 911. I was raised to keep family business to myself and never involve the police unless it was an emergency. But here I was plotting revenge. Calvin really had me fucked up! Twisted! And all of the above. Who in the hell did he think he was shooting up my house? Especially, in front of the kids and my mother.

Oh shit! I got a plan, I told myself as the thought of Calvin shooting up the house in front of the kids and mother brought a devilish grin to my face.

Momma and the kids were in Joy's room doing what? I don't know and I didn't care. I yelled for them like a drill sergeant. "Front and center!" They immediately filed in. Even Momma came limping in.

Momma was fifty-seven, but looked good for her age. I got all my features from her. She had fine hair: long, thick, and black. I lucked up and got her grain of hair. She had the glow of a woman in her mid-forties. She did mighty good with herself until her arthritis started acting up. Her leg gave her the most problems in the worst way. When I was around twelve, she got into it with my father over some bullshit and started chasing him around the projects with a baseball bat in the middle of the street. She never went to the doctor to get it checked out. Inflammation started to build up and eventually it turned into arthritis. I had the same man problems as Momma, but mine were worse, and I was about to eliminate my main headache.

Momma and the kids took a seat on the couch. I went right to work. "Okay, I want to know what everybody just saw a minute ago?"

Joy raised her hand first. "Well, Daddy was talking to me and my sister when you came outside fussing. Y'all exchanged words. Then, Daddy ignored you and started back-talking to us. You got mad. Y'all started arguing over the house. Then, your boyfriend that nobody likes came outside and tried to make Daddy leave his property. Daddy pulled out his gun and started shooting. He shot twice . . ."

I could have slapped the shit out of Joy. The little bitch was forever taking her father's side. She said everything without even blinking an eye. I couldn't stand her. She was the female version of her father. I snapped. "No, bitch! This is what happened!"

I ended up mixing the truth with a little fiction. I told them to say their father popped up out of nowhere drunk and high with a gun in his hand. He was mad because I filed for child support. We were separated, waiting on a divorce, and my boyfriend had moved in with us I told him to leave, but he refused. Then, my boyfriend asked him to leave. He ended up firing twice at my boyfriend.

After I gave everyone the run down on how I wanted them to say what had happened, I asked, "Everyone understand?" I specifically looked at Joy. The room filled with 'yeses'. Joy nodded briskly.

I picked up the phone and did what I had to do. "Nine-one-one, I'd like to report a shooting. My husband just shot up my house. Can you please send some squad cars over here immediately? Thank you."

CALVIN

19

I entered Angel's house and tossed my gun on her glass table. I was surprised it didn't break. I was now drunk as a skunk and teetering like drunken sailor. The only thing on my mind was to fuck the shit out of Angel and fall asleep. Angel appeared asleep when I arrived in her room, but she was wide awake with the lights off.

"Did I wake you?'

"Yes, you did!"

"Well, too bad because I'm 'bout to fuck the shit outta you, girl"

"Calvin, have you been drinking?"

"Yes. And I'm drunk as a drunk leaving a free tequila party. However, girl, this 'bout to be the wildest sexcapade you've ever had, cuz my boy is really ready to kill some shit. Like Young Jeezy say, "I'm 'bout to tear dat pussy up". You know what I mean?"

I was drunk and talking shit. Angel glanced at me and said, "Yeah, whatever. Show me what you working with." To be a doctor she was a freak. I thought I was going to wear her out, but she hopped on top of me, and we went at it. Easy Jesus had me long and strong. Angel gyrated her hips and womb on my dick like there was no tomorrow. Her pleasure box was fat and juicy. To be a little woman - five-foot-two with a measurements of 36C-22-40, she was thicker than a Snickers. We changed position after she rode me like a jockey at the Kentucky Derby.

Terry Wroten

She stood up and turned on the lights. Her body was flawless. Beautiful. I asked myself, *Damn, how did you crack her?* Angel was too good to be true. But here I was drunk and acting like it was our first sexual encounter.

She led me to her bathroom, where she had a floor-to-ceiling mirror mounted to the wall. She bent slowly, grabbed her ankles, and exposed her fat, moist pussy from the back. My boy immediately went from a semi-erect eight-and-a-half to a fully erect nine-and-a-half. I slowly penetrated her from the back while looking at her facial expressions in the mirror. She bit down on her bottom lip. She made every fuck face there was as I proceeded to pound. Our bodies sang joyfully as I held her hips, pushing myself deeper inside her. With her hands still locked at her ankles, she backed her ass into my thrusts. I don't know how she did it, but it felt good. Our bodies started to match each other's pace. She moaned. I moaned. Sounds of pleasure filled the room. Just as I thought I was about to explode, Easy Jesus wouldn't let me. I started pumping harder. I fucked her from the back like an inmate who'd just been released from prison. She sighed and yes-ed. Cries of "fuck me harder", "yes", and "don't stop" escaped her mouth until she climaxed. It was over from there. Her back went out. However, Easy Jesus was still in my system. I was not done as of yet. I laid her on the bathroom floor, missionary style, and proceeded to penetrate. She protested "Calvin, wait. You are killing me."

I frowned. "You are being a poor sport. You get yours, but I can't get mines."

"Okay. I got a better idea."

Angel got on her knees, grabbed my boy by the base, and smiled. "I haven't done this in a long time."

I chuckled. "Yeah right. You had my toes curling the other night."

Her mouth was hot and wet. Her jaw bones were super-strong. She was vicious. My knees started to buckle and my toes started to curl. I started inhaling, exhaling. It was getting intense. I wrapped my hands

Girl, I Had Enough!

behind her head and shoved my boy down her throat. She gagged, but stayed at it. I knew when I got light-headed and my heart felt like I was having a heart attack that I was about to explode. I removed my dick from her mouth and immediately inserted it back into her pleasure box. She protested "Baby, I'm sore." I didn't care. After all the bullshit and drama she'd been through with me, this doctor was about to be mine forever. I exploded. My fluids filled her in lump sums. I just knew I fecundated her.

I smiled inwardly, kissed her on the forehead, and said, "Angel, I love you. Wherever you are in this world, you will always be my girl."

I used her own words against her. She smiled and playfully mushed her index finger into the middle of my forehead. "Calvin, I told you that two years ago. So what is it? The liquor or the blow job?"

I chuckled. "None of the above. Baby, I'm sincere. So sincere!"

She was smiling like the cat who stole the canary. She leaned forward and kissed me on the lips. My boy was still inside her. He was shrinking rapidly, but I decided to let him sit an extra two or three minutes. I wanted all my juices in her. Plus, she was warm and tight. I didn't want to leave this position. I was loving it.

Just as the thought crossed my mind, she shoved me off of her. "Calvin, can we please take this back into the bedroom? This bathroom floor is killing me."

I sucked my teeth and leapt up. I jokingly said, "You know, you complain a lot about how everything is killing you. I thought you was a doctor."

"I am," she said as I helped her from the floor with one hand. She playfully popped me in the stomach with her backhand and grabbed my boy. She had a firm grip on it. "But sometimes you make feel like I'm dying."

I smiled. "And you make me feel like living and enjoying life."

We made it back into the bedroom and got under the covers.

"Calvin, I have a question?" she informed me.

91

Terry Wroten

I asked myself, *Oh shit, what I do now?"* but replied "Shoot."

"Do you need someone to talk to? I ask because I am no fool. I have my doctorate degree and have studied physiology for a very long time. That coupled with my life's experiences make me a great judge of character. You have always been true to your word, and I am proud to have you as my man. But I must know what's on your mind, because you do not drink. And by the way, you were killing me. I'm starting to think you popped one of them sex pills . . ."

I smiled. "What, Ecstacy?"

"Yes. Ecstacy, the new drug these kids are rapidly falling victim to. The other day they rushed a kid into the hospital. He was only twelve and had popped five pills at once, talking about he was horny."

I chuckled. "Naw, honey, I didn't and don't pop pills. But I do have a lot on my mind."

Angel and I lay in bed talking the whole night. I told her everything that had occurred throughout the day. She laughed when I told her I was inches away from killing Alice. "Calvin, you weren't going to kill her. She's the mother of your children."

I laughed to myself thinking about how I was really out of character, but Tupac said it best: "I ain't no killa, but don't push me."

"Angel, a black man can only take so much. But I'm glad shit didn't go as I planned, because my black ass would be in jail."

"Yeah. And I wouldn't know what to do. Probably go crazy or something."

I kissed Angel on the neck, then down to her cheek and lips. "No, you wouldn't. You'd hold strong like the strong black woman you are."

Angel and I talked each other to sleep. I felt there was no other woman in the world for me. I thanked Shalon a thousand times in my head. As we dozed off to sleep, I told myself, "Damn, I love this woman!"

ANGEL

20

Buuuuzzzzzzzzzz! Buuuuuzzzzzzzzz!

It was 5:30 in the morning. Calvin and I had just rested our eyes. I wondered why in the hell Larry, the security guard, was buzzing me? I wasn't expecting company. It was too early in the goddamn morning to be having company! I leapt up from under the covers, furious. I didn't want to wake Calvin, but Larry better have had a good enough reason to be buzzing repeatedly. He at times, accidentally hit the buzzer. That was because he was a young man who hung out with his boys during the day and worked the graveyard post to sleep and get paid at the same time. But this was no accident; the buzzer was going off repeatedly.

"What, Larry?' I said into the intercom in a not-so-pleased tone.

Larry replied, "Ms. Wright, I don't mean to bother you, but a dozen or so police cars are headed your way . . ."

My eyes widened.

"I tried to hold 'em off while I got you on speaker, but they got a warrant to search your house. And if I didn't let 'em in, they were going to arrest me for obstructing justice or something like that."

As soon as Larry finished his sentence they came. And when I say came, I mean CAME! The first thing I heard was a big BOOM! The house rattled like 7.3 earthquake. Then, I heard a lot of noise. They were screaming any and everything that came to mind. I guess this was to frighten, discombobulate, and upset, because I was all three.

My heart skipped a beat or two as they batter-rammed my door down and came in with their guns drawn, like they were looking for a serial killer or rapist. They forced me to the ground. "Get down! Get down!" I did as I was told. I lay on my stomach facing the bedroom while one of the officers grabbed my arms and cuffed me. This was a nightmare come true. I'd never envisioned myself being treated as such. I'd seen people on Cops, but going through the process myself was horrifying. I felt powerless and violated. Tears flooded my eyes. I didn't know why I was being treated so harshly. Then, one of the officers yelled, "Found him!"

I looked on as the officers pounced on Calvin while he was still in bed. Then, I heard a loud SMACK! Another officer yelled, "He's resisting!" The one who had me pinned down with his knee in my back leapt up and ran into the room, followed by an entourage of other officers. They had shields and Tasers in their hands.

I couldn't see much but men in dark uniforms with pistols dangling at their side, black boots, black helmets, and badges. I tried to look and see Calvin, but all I could see was his feet jerking up and down. Then, I realized they were zapping him. I heard the electric currents shooting into Calvin's body.

I sobbed, "Stop it! Stop it!"

I thought they were going to kill Calvin. I yelled and sobbed at the same time. I felt not only were they violating me, they were trying to steal my heart. I wanted to get up and help Calvin, but I couldn't. I was cuffed. I just yelled, "Stop it! Please! You guys are going to kill him!"

A few minutes after they stopped zapping Calvin, it seemed like everything fell still and quiet. I glanced at Calvin's feet. They were pointing straight up. I thought he was dead. I started yelling, "You guys killed him! You guys killed him!" My heart stopped. I couldn't breathe. I started hyperventilating. My body went into convulsions. I heard one

Girl, I Had Enough!

of the officers yell, "Get EMT in here! She's hyperventilating."

"Whatta fuck y'all do to my girl!" Calvin yelled, pumping blood back into my heart. He was alive! I was alive! I told myself, "Okay. Lola, relax. Breathe out your nose. Calm down. He's alive. It's going to be all right."

Calvin stuttered, "Angel, you all right?" He was suffering from the after-effects of being zapped by umpteenth volts of electricity.

I slowed my breathing down and replied, "Calvin, I'm worried. I'm scared. Are you all right?"

Calvin stuttered again, "Yeah I'ma be all right. They roughed me up. And ah-ah Tased me."

One of the officers said, "That's because you punched my partner in the face."

EMT arrived. They asked me, "Are you all right, ma'am?"

I replied "I'm a doctor. I'm okay."

They rushed over to Calvin in the room. The officer who had called the medics for me widened his eyes. He was the same one who had cuffed me. After hearing my occupation, he rushed over to me. "Ma'am, let me explain . . . "

Come to find out, Calvin was wanted for attempted murder. I couldn't believe it. Now, they were adding resisting arrest and battery on a peace officer. They found Calvin's gun in my living room and said it was the gun used in the crime. I furrowed my brows. "There was no crime committed. He didn't shoot any one."

The officer threw his hands in the air. "Well, that's why it's attempted murder, and not murder. His wife filed the report and we have three witnesses. Two are his own kids, and the other is his wife's mother, so we're going to take him down and book him with these charges after the medics get done with him."

I sighed. "Well, can I at least talk to him before you guys take him?"

I started sobbing again. The officer granted me three minutes after EMT left. They walked Calvin out of the room.'His hands were cuffed behind his back. He was bruised up a little bit. I walked to him and wrapped my arms around him. I kissed him on the lips and told him, "I LOVE YOU."

He replied, "I love you too." He kissed me passionately on the lips. "I need you to stay strong. Dry them eyes. I didn't do nothing, so we'll get through this. But I need you to call Byrd. Tell him it's an emergency, come get me! He's in trial right now, so you have to call Shalon first to get him on his emergency line."

I nodded. "I got you, baby." I kissed Calvin one last time and held him tight. I did not want to let him go. Letting him go felt like putting half of my heart under the gun and playing Russian roulette.

"All right, Ms. Wright, we gots to go," the officer who granted me the three minutes said.

My mind was made up. They were going to have to take me to jail with them. I was not going to let Calvin go. Then, the flood gates broke again.

I cried. "No. Please, don't take him." They just didn't understand how much I loved Calvin. Yes. I was the other woman, next woman, or whatever they wanted to call it, but I knew the real story. And I knew that ghetto bitch was lying. I couldn't live with the fact Calvin was going to jail over her trifling ass. But I had to pull myself together before I got too out of character. I was a boss lady. I had to make things happen how I wanted them, not how they fell.

Calvin backpedaled from the embrace. "Baby, come on, stay strong like I told you. Let these people do their jobs. I'll be out as soon as you get in contact with Byrd."

"Do you want me to put up your bail?" I asked.

He shook his head. "No. Byrd will have everything under control. I just want you to stop crying and smile. Matter of fact, smile for me."

I forced a smiled.

"See, that's the Angel I know." He kissed me on the forehead. "And I'm sorry for all this chaos and the embarassment." He turned to the

Girl, I Had Enough!

officers and said, "Let's go." They escorted him out of the house.

My neighbors had gathered in large numbers outside. Nothing ever went on in our community. This was the most action they were ever going to see. Some people even had their cameras out. My neighbor, Connie, walked over to me as they put Calvin in the back of a squad car. I stood outside my house wiping tears from my eyes.

"Lola, what happened?" she asked. "I know Calvin didn't do nothing crazy. Did he?"

Connie, her husband, and their family were the only other black folks on my block in the gated community. Shalon and Byrd lived around the corner, but I knew I had to contact them through their place of employment. Shalon was an attorney-at-law just as Byrd was, so I knew I had to contact their law firm.

"No. He didn't do nothing crazy," I told Connie. "It's just his drama-queen wife and frivolous acts."

Connie nodded. She knew all about Calvin's wife. One day, the two of us were out shopping and I ran into Ms. Ghettofied herself. She immediately started getting boisterous about how I had better leave her husband alone and whatnot. I gave her the cold shoulder and told Connie to come on. I explained Calvin's whole situation to Connie, so she knew about Drama Queen and all the antics she pulled.

Connie replied, "Well, if you need me to watch your house while you go to the police station or anything, just lift up your door to obstruct entrance, and I'll watch your house."

That was all I needed to hear. I agreed and told Connie I needed her to do just that. I ran back into the house, slid on some sweats, tennis shoes, and a T-shirt, and was right behind the squad car that was taking Calvin to jail.

97

BYRD

21

I was in court waiting for the verdict to be read. I'd been in trial exactly eight weeks fighting a murder case for my client, Melvin Dixon. Melvin was a childhood friend who hung with Rah, Calvin, my brother Steel, and I when we were eleven, twelve, and thirteen. My brother got killed at the age of thirteen when I was twelve. Steel and Melvin were best friends. We were all thick as thieves back then. However, on the low, Steel and Melvin joined the Crips. They did not tell anyone. I guess they felt the twins and I wasn't old enough to know.

After my brother got killed, two years later Melvin was arrested for double murder on the guys who were supposed to have been the shooters on my brother's case. He was found guilty in 1984 on both counts. By 1994, on an appeal, the Supreme Court dropped one of the murders on technicalities that the presiding judge ruled unjust and unconstitutional. About this time, I had just passed the bar. I was already helping Melvin with his case while in school. He was fighting it himself, and was doing a hell of a job considering he was incarcerated. But due to his situation, he couldn't do or get everything he needed to fight such a case. I decided to take the case pro-bono fresh out of college.

It had been thirteen years since I started on the case, and twenty-four since Melvin got taken off of the streets. He got married in 1983. It was 2007. I finally got the courts to grant Melvin a re-trial and this was it.

Terry Wroten

Thirteen years of hard work. Let's see if it paid off?

As the court clerk read the verdict, I stood beside Melvin with fingers crossed . . .

"We the jury find Melvin Dixon . . ."

The clerk paused. It seemed like forever. I wanted to scream, "Lady, please hurry up!" But she said the words I wanted to hear: "NOT GUILTY."

The verdict was in. The trial was over. Melvin and I pulled through. Our supporters applauded in joy. I clenched my fist like "yes". Melvin hugged me tight. He was now stress-free. I was stress-free. And now, Melvin was a free man.

"Ladies and gentlemen of the jury, thank you for your time and service. You are now dismissed of your duty." The judge dismissed the jury and acquitted the case. I glanced over at the DA; he was fuming. If looks could kill, I would have been as dead as a doorknob.

The jury was relieved. It was written all over their faces. You could tell none of them wanted to sit in the box. This was why I picked them. I didn't want a jury of retired folks who didn't have nothing else to do. This would have made the case more difficult.

After the jury rushed out of the courtroom, the judge declared Melvin a free man and the case closed. I sat through the final words of the proceeding on cloud nine. Winning a case such as Melvin's would boost any attorney's confidence. I was so happy, I envisioned myself at Red Light District doing the two-step with a few dancers. But that vision didn't last too long.

I was walking out of the courtroom when I got the call. My secretary brought me her cell phone. "Mr. Davis, your wife is on the phone. She say it's an emergency."

I grabbed the phone. "Shalon, what's the emergency? You all right?"

"Baby, Calvin, just got indicted on attempted murder, resisting arrest, and assault on a peace officer . . ."

Girl, I Had Enough!

Shalon was talking nonstop and too fast for my taster, so fast I had to slow her down. She was in trial herself. She was fighting a high-profile civil case. I knew this was bad timing, so I just asked, "Where they have him?" Shalon told me they had him at Newton Division. I was there in no time.

On my way to Newton, I told myself, "If ain't one friend, it's the next. You Negros best be glad somebody decided to go and stay in school."

I arrived at the station and found Dr. Lola Wright seated in the lobby, knees to chest and palms covering her face. She looked a hot mess. I asked, "What happened?"

Lola broke down. She had always been the type of person who carried her emotions on her shoulders and who cried readily for very little reason. I took her into my arms. She sobbed. I hugged her tight. Lola was a strong, yet fragile woman. "Tell me what you know, Lola," I said, "So I could at least have a clue as to what's going on."

"I don't know," she sobbed. "We were asleep. Larry kept buzzin', trying to tell me they were coming. But by the time he told me, they were already knocking down my door with the battering ram. I was forced to the floor, handcuffed, and victimized. They ran into my room and pounced on Calvin. They Tasered him because they said he was resisting arrest, but I don't know how? He was in his own home, asleep, when they came pouncing on him. But come to find out, Alice filed a fictitious report on him saying he tried to kill her boyfriend because he was drunk and high and whole lot of other crap."

As Lola explained what she knew, the family started to file in. First came Rah and Zena, then Trey and Sheila and Sheila's dyke-ass sister. I didn't have anything against lesbianism, but homegirl was too fine to be a lesbian. However, I was off the market. I just felt bad for the brothers who was on the market. After them, a few other family members rolled in, but I was already at the sign-in desk waiting for a detective to come talk to me.

101

Terry Wroten

The detective who was assigned Calvin's case, surprisingly, had the same last name as me. Detective Davis led me to the interrogation room where they had Calvin sitting under a bright light, handcuffed to a chair. As soon as I walked in, he stated, "Man, tell these muhfuckas to uncuff me and get this bright-ass light outta my face."

I looked at Detective Davis and asked, "What is this, some torture chamber?"

Detective Davis stuttered and came up with some nonsense, saying, "Officers feared taking the cuffs off because Calvin had assaulted one of them."

Calvin yelled, "Muhfucka, I didn't assault no one! I was asleep when you bitches came pouncing on me . . ."

I cut Calvin off with my hand. I shook my head at the detective. "Well, detective, before we go any farther, can you please uncuff my client? I assure you, there will be no altercations. And if I may, may I have a word with my client outside this interrogation room, for a law-yer-client talk?"

Detective Davis agreed. He didn't want to, but he had to! As he removed the cuffs from Calvin's wrist, I opened the door so we could step out into the hallway. I knew the interrogation room was wire-tapped. And codes don't matter. The courts got snitches who teach their experts everything. Best believe if I would have asked what happened in there, and he went to codes - "That bitch. Blah, blah, blah did blah, blah, blah, blah. Nahmean?" the expert would have come to court and rephrased everything Calvin said word for word and ended with "know what I mean?"

When we got to a secluded spot in the hallway, I said, "First, before I ask what happened, let me tell you, Melvin got found not guilty. Calvin, we won."

Calvin let out a deep breath. He forced a smile. He was happy for our childhood friend. But now he had his own problems to worry about.

Girl, I Had Enough!

"Man, what happened?" Let me know something. Did you tell these folks anything?"

Calvin screwed his face like "come on, fool, you know me better that". Then, he said, "The only thing I told 'em is I got the right to remain silent and choose my rights."

I nodded in agreement. "Okay. Give me the run down," I informed him.

"Man, I was at the house seeing the kids. Drama Queen come outside with her crap, and we exchange words. Her boyfriend come out the house looking like Tookie Williams. He try to play Captain Save-a-Hoe and push up on me. I ask the man, please, don't step up to me in front of my kids and disrespect me. He do just that. I draw down. Now, you know you don't pull a gun on a man without using it, but as soon as I'm 'bout to get off, Joy jumped in the way, so I shot twice toward the air, hitting the house."

I nodded. "Okay. Now, how we get here?

Calvin shook his head disbelievingly. "That's the muhfuckin problem. That bitch really going out of her way to drive me crazy." Calvin paused. Tears started to run freely out of his eyes. He was hurting from within. The next thing he would tell me will have any righteous man/father in tears. "Man, that bitch even had the twins lie on me. She tried to make Joy do the same, but Joy told the truth on her report. Man, knowing she's turning my kids against me hurt more than being in here. This shit is crazy."

I patted Calvin on the back. I felt his pain. He was a father who took pride in his children. For Alice to use his kids as pawns and against him as such was a blow below the belt. All I could say at that very moment was, "Come on, let's post your bail and fight this from the streets. Don't let the devil get to you, bruh."

RASHEED

22

They released Poppa from the hospital a few days after his heart attack. He was okay. I was pushing down Manchester headed to his house. I stopped at Ralph's grocery store on Western and Manchester first. I had to pick up some groceries that Momma had asked me to pick up. I pushed through the aisles, filling the shopping cart. The list of items Momma asked me to get was front and back. I thought it was never going to end. I had to get items like green peas, wheat bread, Cheerios with no sugar, and diet soda. Just what the doctor ordered. Poppa was on a strict diet, and Momma was a true soldier when it came to her being Bonnie to Poppa's Clyde.

After I checked off every item on the list, I waited in line. The line was long. I hated shopping for this very reason. I picked up a black-orientated magazine to waste time. I forgot the name. I found a column that caught my attention. It was a Q and A in the nature of a Dear Abby. Some dude from New Jersey wrote: *I cheated on my wife. I think she senses that something is going on with me. She ain't say nothing yet, but I think she knows. Should I tell her or not?*

The columnist responded: *Have you lost your mind! Confessions are for Usher. No matter what she says or think, keep your mouth shut. She will never forgive you, and she will never forget. I'm a woman, I know. Your wife will use it against you, even to get her some dick elsewhere.*

Terry Wroten

You were the one who cheated. Brother, I will tell you that you will not gain anything by confession but a headache. Keep your mouth closed. Take that shit to the grave with you. Even do a Shaggy: "It wasn't me . . ."

I laughed to myself. Homegirl was keeping it real. I even thought about how Calvin just gave up so quickly when Charlene called Alice years back to destroy their marriage. I was mad at my brother for weeks, because niggas don't just give up that easy. Even when caught in the pussy, the first thing that comes out a nigga's mouth is "let me explain". Shit, Calvin didn't even deny a damn thing! And just like the columnist wrote, Calvin confessed, and Alice was using his one mistake against him to get her some dick. And it had been fourteen years since the incident, so the columnist was right, a woman will never forgive or forget. Look at all the bullshit Alice was putting Calvin through. Drama Queen even went as far as getting him locked up and having his daughters give statements against him.

I shook my head from the thought. I needed to read that column. I was in the same predicament as old boy, so I felt him. Just as I closed the magazine and bumped up in line, someone tapped me on the shoulder.

"Excuse me, sir." I turned around to see who it was. "Do you be on Facebook?"

I didn't immediately reply. I backpedaled, sizing the woman up to see if I recognized her. She could have been one of my friends.

"Do you go by the name DickGameProper?"

I arched my brows, really trying figure out who this was. She was beautiful. I mean, drop dead gorgeous. I knew I would have remembered her if we had corresponded with each other or anything of that nature. I kept account of all the beautiful women I mingled with on Crackbook. Well, I thought I did. I figured it was Zena running game. She stayed trying to catch a nigga in a lie or something.

I lied, "Naw that ain't me."

Girl, I Had Enough!

"Come on now, Rasheed. Look me in the eyes and tell me that ain't you."

"Oh shit! Tiffany."

It was my first fling from Crackbook. She looked new and improved. She looked damn good two years back. But her new Halle Berry hairdo and look make her look different. Back then, she had long silky blonde hair with dark streaks. Her hair now was jet-black and complimented her yellow skin. She even looked a little thicker and more toned, like she hit the gym daily.

I nodded. "Yep. And you must've finally got rid of Workaholic."

Tiffany let out a deep breath. "Whoo! You still remember that?"

I wanted to reply, "Hell yeah! You were my first Crackbook jump off," but I just nodded. "You damn right."

I asked, "So what are you doing with yourself lately?"

She poked her chest out, proud of herself. "Well, I'm a bestselling author right now. I'm working on the follow-up to my first book. It's called Freaky Extortions: When Nature Calls. It's a sexy book. Erotica. I followed Zane's lead and wrote a lot of short sex stories. Matter of fact, you will like it. I got an extra copy you can have in the car."

I didn't know what to say. Tiffany had come up since our one night stand. We waited in line, talking. She was right behind me. After we made it to the cashier and paid for our groceries, we walked to her car. She only had a brown bag of groceries. The contents in the bag indicated to me that she was either on a vegetarian diet or a vegetarian.

"You didn't tell me you was a vegetarian."

"At that time, I didn't feel you needed to know. Remember, I said no strings attached."

I nodded.

"Yes. I'm a vegan. I eat a lot of nourishing foods: white rice, peas, carrots, turnips, and I drinks lots of water. However, I cheat at times, like eating cookies, potato chips, ice cream, and maybe some pork chops."

Terry Wroten

"Yeah. I was 'bout to say, 'cause with a body like yours, you eating more than some goddamn peas, carrots, and turnips."

We shared a laugh. She said, "Well, I'm trying to make the body last. I hit the gym or do exercises with the TV set. You know, a little Tae-Bo here and there. Might have to kick a nigga's ass one day."

She threw a few phantom punches. I fell out in laughter. "Girl, I know you ain't planning on whipping nobody throwing punches like that."

She smiled. "No. I'm a lover not a fighter. I was just playing with you."

"So who you lovin' right now?" I asked flirtatiously.

She twisted her lips. "Are you flirting with me?" She handed me the book, then quickly snatched it back. "Boy, you got me moving so fast I forgot to sign it for you. And don't read what I'm 'bout to write until I'm out of your sight."

She handed me the book again after she wrote a few lines and signed it. I looked at the cover. It read: Freaky Extortions: When Nature Calls. Erotica by Tiffany Childs, a.k.a NaughtyGirl69.

I smiled. "Tiffany Childs. Now, I know your real name."

She smacked her lips. "Don't act like you don't know. Oh, you were too busy tryna get some, you forgot."

"You said no strings attached."

"Yeah, you right about that," she replied. "But I sure do remember your name, Mr. Rasheed 'Rah" Williams."

We exchanged words and laughter for a cool minute, but we both had to get going. "Oh, before we part, can I at least get a hug and your number? Or is it still no strings attached now that you are separated?"

"Shit, I should be asking you that," she said sarcastically. "You are the married one, not me. Anyhow, my number is in the book so you won't lose it. And yes you can get a hug. Just don't try to get too touchy, you might turn me on."

We hugged, said our farewells, and went our separate ways.

TIFFANY

23

*O*h my God, I thought as I drove off. I had finally run into Rasheed's fine ass after two-and-a-half years of not seeing him. And he looked good! Better than the night of our one night stand, when he beat my pussy into a coma. He had a wifebeater on, showing off his well-defined biceps and tattoos. He had a portrait of his daughter on his forearm and a scroll under it. I just loved his tattoo. It was a very fine piece of artwork and it fitted Rah to a T. Inside the scroll read:

My precious daughter. For you I give the world. My last breath. And my love. FOREVER. Daddy loves you. Maryam Carrie Williams, OCTOBER 28TH 2004 TO ETERNITY.

I had been fascinated with that tattoo since day one. It gave him that thug appeal, but still showed his gentle, loving, caring side. I also couldn't help but notice them eyes of his. They brought a sparkle to his glow. He kept his hair wavy like a bee-hive and was comely in appearance. I smiled all the way home. And from Los Angeles to Rialto, I was smiling a very long time..

When I made it home, I couldn't get Rah off my mind. He had my mind blown more than he knew it. I tried to clean, exercise, read, and write to get Rasheed off of my mind, but I couldn't. I was just hoping he'd call so we could get together again. I knew he was married, but I was willing to accept that fact as long as I could get a few one–on-ones with him every now and then. I mean, I couldn't lie to myself, he really lived up to his name. DickGameProper fit him to a T. This coupled with his tongue game would have had any woman with an abnormal uncontrollable sex drive, stealing from her momma and fiending like a crack addict for his dick.

It was a quarter after midnight when my brain finally let me catch some Z's, but that was only after I'd knocked out a few pages to my sequel. I wrote:

Subject: Mr. DickGameProper . . .

Today, I was awoken by my digital alarm clock at six in the morning. I had a long day ahead. I had to hit the local YMCA. I signed up with my sister, Alma, and a few other people to take up an aerobic class. Then, I had to be in LA before twelve to meet my attorney at the courthouse. I was worried shitless about that. I didn't know who was going to be awarded what. We all know my husband worked 24/7 and was the bread winner, but since my book hit the best seller's list, his lawyer been asking for alimony. All of a sudden, Mr. Workaholic ain't working no more. So I was nervous about that. I also planned on going to my momma's house, since I was going to be in the city and stopping by Simply Wholesome on Slauson and Overhill, to get some supplemental vitamins and good food. Simply Wholesome is the best nutritional restaurant in Los Angeles. Plus, it's black-owned. I had to support my people, because it's not too many black-owned businesses in Los Angeles no more. The Asians and the Mexicans are buying up any and everything. Blacks are not doing nothing but packing their shit and moving elsewhere; so for the few black owned businesses still left, I try my best to support.

Anyhow, the alarm clock went off at six. I leapt up from under the covers and got dressed. I made it to the Y about seven, right on time for the aerobic class. Alma had arrived before me and was bent at the waist, holding her ankles, looking between her legs. I slapped her on the ass.

Girl, I Had Enough!

"Hey, girl!"

Alma stayed in position, looking at me between her legs. "Uh-hmm, do that again. That's how Todd was smacking it last night."

I cracked a one-sided smile. "You freaky bitch."

Todd was our gay aerobic instructor. He was fine as hell! Alma and I had a bet going—who could get the dick first? And who can turn Todd back straight? Buy Todd wasn't having it. One day, he just flat out told us, "I'm strictly dickly. I like getting mines beat just like y'all, so ladies, stop flirting. Y'all ain't R. Kelly. Okaaaaaaay?"

After our one hour class aerobics, Alma and I headed to our cars. I was trying to get her to ride with me, but come to find out she had a date for brunch with Curtis, the neighborhood dope man. Knowing her, she was going to suck his dick then rob him dry. My sister was scandalous and had no shame in her game. She believed if a man was stupid enough to fall for her trap, he needed to be played. She said, "If a nigga can't read between the lines and see that I'm a larcenous and devious bitch, that's on him."

I waved her off. Girl, I don't want to hear yo' so-called game, because once one of your victims find out what you are doing, you gon' wish you never done it."

"So what make you all so self-righteous now? How you did your husband, you shouldn't say shit."

I agreed. I did do my husband wrong, but it was only because he neglected me for his job. "Yeah, you right. That's why I'm stressed the hell out now. I hope my lawyer don't tell me no bullshit, 'cause then I'm really fucked. I don't wanna lose the house and everything. I'm so scared."

"Girl, you going to be all right. I just got this feeling everything is going to go your way today. And you know when I be having good vibes, good things happen. Anyhow, call me when you get in."

I left the Y, went home, and took a quick shower. When I made it to the courthouse, it was right around noon. My attorney was waiting for

111

me outside. She must have seen that I was nervous by the way I walked, because as soon as I approached, she said, "Smile, girl, the world ain't bout to end." I had Bernice Gold as my lawyer. She was a sista and down-to-earth. She knew more rap and ghetto songs than me. I liked sistagurl, as I called her.

"Anyhow, look, I'm in trial. I got these settlement papers I want you to go over. Your husband is willing to let you have everything. He just wants his art collection and a few other things you said you don't care about. I think either his high-priced lawyers are getting more out of him than you could ever ask for, or his new girlfriend is rushing him to finalize the divorce so they can get married. Whatever it is, we are winning."

I let out a deep breath. I was relieved. Breezing over the settlement papers, I saw my husband was letting me keep the house, the car and everything that I asked for. Shit, this was better than I thought. I started smiling like the cat who stole the canary. I could not have asked for nothing more. I didn't expect him to give up so easily. What was that saying he used to say? Oh! "That's small shit to a giant, you dig?" I guess that's how he took it. I don't know. But I know one thing, I won!

"Well, if you want to settle, which I know you do, lets meet back here next week."

I agreed, said goodbye, and got on with the rest of my day. I ended up stopping by Momma's house. She needed me to pick up a few items from Ralph's before I drove home. I decided to hit the one on Manchester and Western. And y'all won't believe who I bumped into? Yes. Mr. DickGameProper himself. I spotted his fine ass a mile away. He had on a wifebeater, looking like a complete sex symbol. Y'all know from book one how he put it down, so yes! Nature was calling. I became immediately moist between the legs. I had to double-take to make sure it was him before I approached. I couldn't believe it was him standing in line reading a magazine. Or acting like he was reading one. I recognized his tattoo off top and told myself, "Damn! God finally sent my dream back to me."

Girl, I Had Enough!

I tapped DickGameProper on the shoulder to get his attention. I asked him if his name was DickGameProper and dif he was on Facebook? He took a step back to get a better look at me, I guess to try to put a name to my face. No telling how many other sluts he done banged up, because he glanced me over and said, "Naw, that ain't me."

He was denying it. I knew he was lying because he was a married man. I called him by his real name and told him to look me in the eyes. Once he did that, he knew exactly who I was. "Oh shit! Tiffany."

I nodded, "Yes."

It was back on from there. I told him about me being a bestselling author and gave him a copy of *Freaky Extortions*. I signed it, wrote my number in it, and told him to read chapter ten, if no other. We all know what chapter ten about, so as I write this, I'm hoping he's reading it.

Well, it's going on the midnight hour and I need my beauty sleep. Hopefully tomorrow I hear from Mr. DickGameProper, so I can finish this chapter off with a *Freaky Extortion*. Y'all know what I mean?

RASHEED

24

At Poppa's house, I sat with him for hours talking about life after his exit. He was on his last lap of life and wasn't too proud with the way I acted while he was hospitalized.

"Son, you are the poster boy of this family," he told me. "If you break, the whole family will break. This is from your mom on down to your sisters and brothers. I've been sick for years now. I didn't tell no one other than your mother. The only reason I told her was because I needed her to understand if I was to just drop dead, she'd still have to raise y'all to be at least half decent people. However, I've lived to see this age where even my grandchildren will remember me. Son, I am not proud of you right now. Look at you! The way you carried yourself at that hospital was not the strong man I raised you to be. Son, you are just letting yourself go. Look at them things sticking out of your shirt pocket . . ."

I glanced down and there they were. A habit I couldn't kick. A habit I'd been secretly hiding. Newports had once again become my best friend.

"I can see it in your eyes, you are going through it. You haven't smoked a cigarette since I made you and your brother smoke ten packs nonstop. Son, you are hurting me in a major way. I didn't' expect you to be so fragile. If I did, I would've named your older brother as my beneficiary and not you. You got to stand tall. You understand?"

"Yes."

"Now what's bothering you? Because it's written all over your face."

I swallowed spit, but spoke my mind. I needed to know why Poppa didn't tell me he had heart disease a long time ago. I thought we were thick as thieves. I was hurt that he didn't confide in me.

I said, "Well, first, I need to know, were you ever going to tell me or us that you were sick? Or were you going to wait 'til the last minute, like now? Poppa, I feel it ain't fair. I just thought that out of all the people in the world, if anything was wrong with you, you woulda told me. I mean, it's all type of things that coulda happened."

Poppa shook his head in defeat. "Son, you are right. But you don't know how hard it has been on me keeping this secret from y'all, especially you. I wanted to tell you so bad, but than again, I'm glad I didn't. Y'all would have been walking around with y'all head down for the last twenty odd years. I do apologize for staying quiet for so long. I just couldn't tell y'all."

I nodded. I understood. Poppa knew what was best, and always had. I just needed to know why he felt he couldn't tell me to move on and feel a sense of relief. While we were talking, I decided to ask Poppa how did he stay faithful to Momma? I needed to know, 'cause I was having problems in that area. And it wasn't that I didn't love my wife. I was just a dog. I liked to explore.

Poppa said, "Well, do you want the truth or a lie?"

"Give me the truth, raw and uncut."

"Well, if you must know, I was never actually faithful to Momma. It ain't that I didn't love her, because anyone in his or her right mind knows Momma is the blood that pumps through this heart. But I was just being a man. It's in our nature to roam. That's why they call us dogs. Also, back in my day, I had so many women around town wanting some of old Poppa Flash. But one thing I did was never brought any of my unfaithfulness home. All my jump-offs knew I was married.

116

Girl, I Had Enough!

Momma was my girl, so if I humped on a female, she knew it was just a wham-bam-thank you ma'am. However, like I always tell y'all, what you do in the dark comes to the light. Momma caught me one day. We had our fallouts. I think you and your brother was no older than five or six. So to answer your questions, no, I haven't always been faithful to your mom. I just never brought none of my bullshit home. Shit, boy, playing with a woman's feelings is like playing Russian roulette. And when she's fed up, it's like throwing a match at a powder keg."

It was a quarter to ten when Poppa and I wrapped up or father to son conversation. I just needed to hear his input on why I loved my wife, but couldn't do her no justice by keeping my dick in my pants. I didn't feel like driving all the way home after our talk, so I decided to crash there. I called Zena and told her I was staying the night. She didn't sound too pleased, but she agreed. I settled in the guest room after Momma cooked a meal for CJ and I.

CJ had moved in with Poppa and Momma after he got into it with Alice over her boyfriend. Alice picked her boyfriend over her son, so CJ got on. He was only seventeen and going through it. He looked so much like Calvin and me, Alice took her anger out on him every time she got mad at his father. And that was everyday. Then, Calvin hated putting up with Alice's drama, so he'd just up and disappear for months. All this, coupled with the gang culture in Los Angeles, and there was no wonder why CJ walked around with a blue bandana in his left back pocket, ran the streets with the Crips, and stayed high as the Trump Towers.

I wanted to sit down and talk to my nephew, but I saw that it would have been a waste of time. He was sitting at the table high, drunk, and everything else, listening to Tupac's *Still I Rise* CD and filling his face with fried chicken, mashed potatoes, corn, rice and sugar, and fresh-squeezed lemonade. Momma cooked up a storm. As CJ bobbed his head with his headphones at top volume, Momma looked at him and shook her head. He was in his own world.

Terry Wroten

"You know, he only acts out because he sees his mom and dad do it," Momma said. "I tell Calvin all the time, he needs to do something, but he be caught up with Alice, he don't see his own goddang son slippin' right before his eyes. Rasheed, you need to talk to him before one of these crazy guys out here kills him. It hurts. He only a baby. He don't know no better."

I nodded in agreement. "Momma, I know. But you already know he ain't gon' listen to me. We'll just be in here fighting. He already thinks he can beat me. This comes from his mama tellin' him he don't got to listen to me when he was younger. You know just as much as Alice hates Calvin, she hates me. But what I will do is talk to Trey. He'll listen to Trey. Calvin already going through it with his case and tryna stay out of jail."

Momma nodded while washing dishes. "See, that's why I be telling y'all, choose the women y'all mess with carefully, 'cause it don't only affect y'all, it affects the whole family."

I nodded. But I honestly was not trying to get caught up in any long conversations with Momma about women and what not. I yawned. "Momma, I hear what you are saying. I'll talk to Trey as soon as I get a chance, but I'm tired. I'm 'bout to take my behind to bed. Anyway, thank you for the lovely meal."

Momma waved me off. "Boy, gon' ahead. I gave birth to you. I wasn't born yesterday. I know you better than you know yourself. I know you don't want to hear an old lady talk all night."

I pecked Momma on the cheek and headed to the guest room. I stretched out on the king-size bed and lay like a dead cockroach looking at the ceiling. This was not the house I grew up in, because I would have slept in the room. Poppa had upgraded to a house in Culver City. It was a big house right off of the city lines. I liked the house, but I missed the one in Leimert Park. Leimert Park was my stomping grounds. Not adding that it was an all-black neighborhood and community.

118

Girl, I Had Enough!

As I lay there, my mind drifted to Tiffany. I couldn't seem to get her off my mind. She was smoking hot. I mean, just plain gorgeous. I was curious to know what she was talking about in her book. I also wanted to call her. I leapt up from bed and ran to my car. I opened my trunk and grabbed the book from under my spare tire. I had it there to keep Zena from finding it.

I settled back into bed and opened the book. Tiffany Childs had signed the first page. She wrote:

Dear Rasheed,

I hope you enjoy. I know you are a busy man, so if you can't read the whole book, at least read chapter ten and tell me what you think and how you feel? My number is (909) 555-4248.

I immediately turned to the table of contents and breezed through a few titles. Some were called "Get Your Freak On", "Supply and Demand", "Smack That", "Buy U A Drink", and "Pussy Popping". The title of chapter ten was "DickGameProper". The page number was 137. I went straight to it and started reading.

It read:

Today I got home from work horny as hell. I was fiending in the worst way. My husband was out of town on business once again and couldn't satisfy me. I was tired of my favorite toy. My fingers were sore. And satisfying myself just wasn't going to work. I needed someone else to play with my pussy. I needed the warmth of a Mandingo inside of me to put out the fire that was burning within. I thought of all the ways I could just fall back and wait 'til my husband got home, then go hard in the paint on his ass. But I couldn't. The cold showers weren't working. The vibrator between my legs wasn't working. I felt hopeless. Then, a light popped on in my head.

Just a week before, I became a member of Facebook. I was sitting at home bored. My husband was gone on business as usual. I heard my co-workers talking about the site at work. I checked it out and fell in love the first day. I made a profile and I chatted with any and everybody. The next day at work, one of co-workers showed me how to navigate the site and add pictures to my page. I did just that. Facebook became my favorite pastime. I stayed on it a week straight, chatting with different folks about current events, social gatherings, new trends, jobs, etc. But today I was on a mission. I was horny as hell and remembered seeing this brother on Facebook who looked like The Game. He was fine as wine. He had a picture on his page that showed everything but his dick. But I envisioned it to be at least a seven. He had spinning waves and a tattoo on his forearm. He had sexy written all over him. I knew off top, one day, he and I was going to be doing the wild thang. Married or not, I was having freaky fantasies about him. I was so pleased with his appearance, I wrote his display name on a piece of paper by my computer. DickGameProper is what he called himself. Shit, that name turned me on even more. If his dick game was proper, that meant he had the total package: body, looks, and dick. WOW! I shivered just from the thought. I needed someone just like him to wipe me down.

I ran to my computer and logged onto Facebook. I immediately found DickGameProper. To my benefit, better yet, our benefit, he was online. I emailed him a raunchy but straight to the point message. "Damn, boy, you got body! I just want to touch it." He replied with a smiley-face wink. I took that as he must have been to my home page, seen my pictures, and was interested. I sent him another message. He sent one back. One thing led to another and he was on his way to spank me. And the good thing was, he was married; I was married. We agreed no strings attached. Shit, I didn't need nothing from this fireman but for him to put out the fire that was burning within.

Mr. DickGameProper arrived at my house an hour after our last email. I'd dimmed lights and popped in a porno. Donnell Jones's *Where I Wanna Be* CD was playing in the background. I had nothing on but a thong and stilettos. I was so horny, my fat and juicy pussy was bulging through the fabric—camel toe fa sho'. I opened the door and smiled.

Girl, I Had Enough!

DickGameProper licked his lips and said, "Damn, baby, you didn't tell me you was going to be in nothing but some stilettos and a thong. Shit, if that's the case, I would have got ass-naked in the car."

"Say no more." I covered his mouth with my right hand and slammed the door with my left. I led him directly to my room. I spun around at the entrance. "You like?"

"You damn right, I like. Legs like Beyonce. Ass like J-Lo."

"Well, get naked."

I was blunt. I was horny. I was fiending. And I didn't need any distractions. And I sho' didn't need to go the technical route of asking a series of questions, and getting a series of answers. Well, not at that moment.

DickGameProper stripped out of his clothes faster than a stripper. And when I saw his Mandingo, I knew I had hit the jackpot. I wanted to be creative. My pussy was throbbing. It instantly wanted to be touched. Unrehearsed and unscripted, I jumped into bed, spread my legs, and started playing with myself. I got off with one hand and held my nipple to my mouth with the other. DickGameProper stood at the edge of the bed, sliding on a condom. He had one hand on his hip and the other stroking his dick. It grew to a pleasurable size eight. He was stroking himself so fast, his tattoo looked like it was going to jump out of his skin onto me. I bit down on my bottom lip, thinking about how his nice piece of man meat was 'bout to tear my pussy up. The thought alone had me fingering myself into oblivion. I started moaning low moan from the pleasure I was giving myself.

"Whooooool."

I sucked in air. "Sssssssssssss . . ."

DickGameProper couldn't just sit back and watch. He hopped in bed with me. He removed my fingers and placed his tongue right on the tip of my clitoris. I arched my back as the warmth of his breath mixed with the stiffness of his tongue worked miracles. He then started fingering me viciously.

"Ooooooooooooooogh!" I moaned. "Aaaaaaaaaaaaaaaagh!"

Terry Wroten

"Yes. Yes. Yes."

"Suck it, baby. Suck it."

"Oh my Gawd! Yes. Right there."

I tried my best to hold back from climaxing. DickGameProper most definitely knew what he was doing with his tongue. I couldn't help but explode when I felt my body lock. I shivered uncontrollably. It felt so good it was over. I squirted. My juices were all over his face when he removed it from between my legs.

"Oh youse a squirter,, huh?" he asked, smiling.

Silence.

I couldn't answer right away. I had to regain my composure. It was my turn to return the favor. I leapt up and grabbed his shaft. I led him to the balcony. It was pouring cats and dogs. I removed the unused condom from his penis as rain and cold air hit our bodies. I brought a pillow along with us so I wouldn't scrape my knees.

"Damn, baby girl, yo' mouth feel so damn good. Make some slurping noises for me."

I locked my jaws, puckered my lips, and started moving my head up and down. I started making slurping noises.

"Ssssllluurp."

"Ssssllluurp."

Occasionally I'd stop and spit, but tonight went nonstop. I relaxed my throat and tonsils and took as much of his Mandingo down my throat as I could. I teased him with the tip of my tongue as I stroked his base and played with his balls with my free hand.

"Ha!" he laughed trying to hide the pleasure I was giving him. His knees buckled. I had him. "Whool-wee! Damn, ma, this shit is the bomb."

I was a pro at giving head. Should have been getting paid at the local college, because my head game was a craft that a lot of chicks needed to study. My routine was bob and weave, stop and tease.

Girl, I Had Enough!

"Aww, hell naw! Baby Girl, I know you ain't stopping. That shit was too bomb. A nigga was just 'bout to nut."

I looked up at DickGameProper, grinning a devilish smile. I still had a firm grip around his shaft. I kissed it and shot, "I know."

He frowned. "Well, man, stop playing and get the job done."

When I stopped teasing DickGameProper and went all out with my head game, I was giving blows to the head like Tyson in the 80's. I didn't stop. I sucked. Sucked. Sucked. And sucked!

"Damn! Yeah. That's it."

"Suck that shit, ma."

"Suck it."

He exploded in my mouth and demanded that I swallow. I did as told. I figured a little protein wouldn't hurt.

My pussy was now on FIRE. I told him to stay put. I ran into the house and grabbed another condom. I put it on him with my mouth. "Stay still," I told him as I did so. I then turned around and got in doggy-style position.

"Are you a freak?" he asked out of nowhere.

I looked over my shoulder, furrowed my brows, and replied, "Whatchu think?"

"It's not good to answer a question with a question. But just because you been acting up since I got here, just do as I say."

Silence.

I didn't say a word. I love a man who can take in charge and bring spontaneity to a sexual encounter. A little excitement and spontaneity made a good combination.

"Toot yo' ass up a little more, relax, and breath in and out slowly."

Oh my God! He's tryna take a bitch's ass. I wanted to protest, but you only live once. My husband tried numerous times; it just didn't work. He didn't know what he was doing, but Mr. DickGameProper did.

Terry Wroten

I did as told. I felt him rip into my shit box. It was painful.

"OH MY GAWD!"

"WAIT! WAIT!"

I tensed up and tried to escape, but he was locked onto me like a pit-bull. Tears rushed to my eyes as he ripped my asshole open. I cried for five minutes before the pain turned into pleasure. Once he got in, it was all good. I'd never felt the pleasure I was feeling as he slowly veered in and out of my ass. The feeling was unbelievable. It was great.

While he stroked my anal, I played with my pussy. *Damn, this some of the best dick I'd done ever had.*

"Fuck me, Big Boy. Fuck me."

I moaned at the top of my lungs. Rain was splashing onto my face. I was huffing and puffing like a dog that'd just ran a five mile race with her owner. I love the anal sex. It was great. But my pussy was screaming for her due.

After he removed his penis from my ass, I couldn't walk. I was sore as hell. But I didn't care how bad I was hurting, I was going to get me some dick.

He carried me to the bed, like Hercules, and laid me down. He got on top of me, missionary style, and slid his Mandingo into my pleasure box; and she rejoiced. He felt so warm inside me. My juices started flowing like Niagara Falls. He started slow, but ended up fucking me wild and rough. He showed me no mercy. And that's how I wanted it. Sounds of pleasure filled the room. He went for what seemed like eternity, pounding away nonstop. I'd never had a man to hit it how he hit it. It was literally wham-wham-wham-wham-wham! All night long until I could not take no more. I moaned and groaned. He was tearing me up. I wanted him to stop. Then, I didn't want him to stop. He was taking me places insanity hide. He took me to la-la land and beyond. He fucked my brains out. I enjoyed myself. I counted, at least five orgasms before we fell asleep.

Girl, I Had Enough!

The next morning when I woke up, he was putting on his jeans getting ready to leave. My pussy was throbbing. Not throbbing because she wanted to be pleased, but because she was hurting! DickGameProper put a beat down on my girl so proper, she was going to be good for a long time. With this knowledge, I couldn't just let Mr. Magic Stick walk out on me. Now I felt bad for not going the technical route and asking the basic series of questions and getting the basic series of answers. However, I did just that. What's your birth name? How long have you and your wife been married? How many kids do you have? What do you do for a living? Blah, Blah, Blah...

DickGameProper ended up telling me his name, but I'd rather not say to protect him and his marriage. However, for the other questions, he simply replied, "No strings attached." He walked out of my house like nothing ever happened. I have not heard or spoke to him since. So DickGameProper, if you ever read this book, holler at your girl, because your dick game is proper, and I'm fiending in a major way . . .

I shook my head after reading chapter ten. Tiffany really put our whole sexcapade in her book. And I respected how she did it. She didn't use any names. I closed her book and fell asleep smiling. I was going to call Ms. Childs first thing in the morning.

ZENA

25

I was determined not to cry. I felt like Mary J. Blige: "I'm not gon' cry. I'm not gon' cry. I'm not gon shed no tears…" I was fed up, tired of being hurt, and tired of cheatin'-ass Rasheed. It had been three long-long months since I found out about his Facebook page. However, I decided to fall back like a real wife should. Poppa was sick and going through his last days of life. I didn't want to make it seem like I was nagging over a website page, so I fell back, hoping to gather more information. His Facebook page was a good clue that he was cheating, but the nigga had everything tight. He was so smart, he gave me the password to his voice message, but it was to a phone he used only for business. I thought he only had one phone, but I would eventually learn he had two spares that he kept in his car. He had me looking like a fool answering and checking his messages only to hear Calvin, Trey, Byrd, or one of his business partners talking business. For a minute, I thought I was really going crazy.

Rasheed ain't cheating on you, girl. You just insecure, I told myself. *You gain an extra twenty pounds and lose all your goddamn self-esteem. Zena, what's wrong with you, girl?*

I shook my head and answered my own question out loud. "I don't know. But I know one thing: I'm not gon' cry no more. A bitch has cried enough. Simple as put, if I catch that nigga this time, I might kill him and the bitch."

I sat in the love seat in our living room, sipping on some Grey Goose, puffing some kush, and watching On-Demand videos, The good thing about On-Demand, you could choose what you want to watch and listen to. I had Keyshia Coles' single "Shoulda Cheated" playing. I rocked slightly from side to side, thinking. I took a long pull off the potent weed and found myself thinking back to the day it all went bad . . .

"Zena, why is that bitch giving you the evil eye?" Jada asked, cracking her knuckles.

She, Sheila, Alice, and I were out shopping at the Beverly Center. We stopped in Lady's Footlocker. Sheila wanted to buy herself a pair of walking shoes. She was getting ready for some gay/lesbian parade. She said she was going to support her sister, but I figured that was a lie. Sheila had gay tendencies. She made lesbian comments all the time. Like one time, she told me, "Man will be man, all men cheat. You don't need a man all he wanna do is cheat then beat, but you get a female and eat-eat-eat." When made such statements I waved her off.

I looked up to see who was giving me the evil eye and spotted the heifer off top. We made eye contact, then she looked off as if she was looking at a pair of shoes. I glanced her over once before turning to Sheila and Alice. The bitch looked familiar. Even the two other chickenheads she was with looked familiar, especially the older one.

I tried hard to put a name to her face, but I couldn't. The look she gave me meant one of two things: we were either fucking the same man, or she was trying to reckon if she knew me. She was copper-tone with full lips and wide hips. She stood no taller than five–foot-five. Her hair was dyed platinum blonde. And she had chestnut eyes. Stripper was written all over her. And Sheila declared it.

"Oh, that's them bitches, Ayana, Diamond, and Deanna. Them bitches work at the club and probably fucking my husband and think I don't know. They probably was staring at me, not you."

Girl, I Had Enough!

"Psst," Jada hissed. "Yeah right! I saw how that bitch with the blonde weave was looking at my sister. She's probably fuckin' Rasheed too."

That was a dagger to my heart to hear my younger sister confirm what I thought. It was like a nightmare turned reality. I'd asked Rah over a thousand times if he was cheating on me? I told him just be a man about it and tell me. For a minute, I thought it could be someone I know, such as my sister. Jada was known to be wild and trifling, so even though she'd always assured me she wasn't fucking Rah, I still knew in the midnight hours, pussy has no face and stiff dick is related to no one.

Alice snapped her neck from side to side. "So what y'all want to do? It's whatever with these bitches." Alice was ghetto wherever she went and was down like four flat tires when it came time to scrap. However, I was too pretty to get any battle scares on my precious face. My father taught Jada and I how to use a gun at a young age. We were somewhat military brats growing up, so every time he came home from overseas, he brought home a new gun. I ended up falling in love with revolvers. They never jammed, and most were small enough to fit in the average purse.

I dug into my Louis Vuitton purse and cocked the hammer to my .50 Cal. Alice's eyes widened. "Girl, I know that's not a gun you packing, because I'll tell you right now. A bitch is with the fisticuffs. I'll take an ass-whippin' or give one or two any day. I'll even take a goddamn assault case. But a bitch ain't' bout to play with no guns and catch a murder. I'm sho' not tryna do no life when I got a nigga whose life I could make miserable, spend all his money, and even get fucked on the side. You could call me Queen Bitch all you want, but I'm sho' not Queen Blasta Bitch."

Sheila poked me in the arm. "Girl, uncock that gun and come on. We gon' confront the one who's staring. Her name is Deanna."

"Now, that's more like it," Alice said, taking off her silver hoop earrings.

129

Terry Wroten

Jada playfully shoved me on the shoulder. "Yeah, you just dying to use your gun since Daddy gone, huh?" A snide grin spread across her face. She slightly opened her purse. "You ain't the only one." She had a chrome nickel-plated .9mm tucked in her Coach bag.

"Hey! Sheila, how you doing, girl? Ain't seen you at the club in a while. Everything all right between you and Dolla?" Diamond asked, smiling.

Dolla was Trey's street name. Sheila dismissed Diamond's fake smile and greeting. She snarled, "You could gon' with all the smiling in my face and fucking my husband behind my back. We just came over here because it seems to us, Ms. Deanna got a staring problem." Sheila turned to me. "Zena, gon' ahead and ask her."

I stepped face to face to Deanna. "Do I know you?" I asked. "Are you fucking my husband or something? 'Cause you staring at me like I stole something from you."

Deanna squinted real tight. "You right. That's what I was trying to figure out, do I know you. You the one come stepping up all in my face. Bitch, do I even know your husband?" She looked at Sheila with a confused look. "Shelia, who the fuck is this bitch?"

I chimed in, "I'm not gon' be too many of your bitches."

Alice, forever ghetto, added, "That's on the real. That's on the hood. We can get it crackin'."

"Look, Sheila," Diamond said, "we just came to get our shop on. We ain't tryna break no nails over no bullshit. We all grown. And we all know men cheat."

Sheila got agitated. "Bitch, we all know that! But that wasn't the question your girlfriend was asked. The question is: why is she staring at her? Is she fucking her husband or something? It's a simple question. Yes or no?"

"First of all, I don't even know who her husband is," Deanna lied. "And second, I wasn't staring at her. I was trying to put a face to you. I knew that I knew you from somewhere, just couldn't figure out where."

Girl, I Had Enough!

My gut feeling told me she was lying. You could tell from her facial expression, Deanna knew exactly who I was. And now I knew exactly who she was.

Sheila said, "Okay that will sum this up. Sorry for the confusion, but I know y'all all fucking my husband. But as always, it's okay. I guarantee y'all, I will have the last laugh. So laugh now, cry later when you ho's be out of a job."

Sheila grinned like she had something up her sleeve. "Come on, y'all. Men and women come a dime a dozen."

After we did our shopping, Sheila dropped Jada and me at my house. Jada hung out and smoked a few blunts with me, but left around ten. She had a booty call and told me she was not about to sit up with me all night while I pouted over a nigga when I could have any nigga I wanted. But what she didn't understand was that I had the nigga I wanted; he just wasn't acting right.

I paced around the house back and forth. Upstairs and downstairs. Our house was too big for me to be in it alone approaching the midnight hour. I was scared. I needed my husband to be there to hold me and let me know everything was all right and to protect me, but the only thing I had to protect me was my gun. I was starting to get used to this. It was going on a year since Rah first ventured out late or didn't coming home at all started. He blamed it on work, business, or falling sleep at one of his brother's houses unintentionally. I believed him the first couple of times, but when it became every other night or day, my suspicions arose. Then, the sneaky shit started, like whispering and giggling on his cell phone in the bathroom. It even got worse when every time he was around me, he immediately answered his phone, but when it came to me, my calls went unanswered. After all this, I knew he was cheating. There were no ifs, ands, or buts about it. He was cheating!

It was a quarter to twelve when I decided to see where he was at. I couldn't stand sitting around the house by myself. Plus, I couldn't sleep. I wanted so badly to ask him about this Deanna bitch to see if I could mix him up by lying and saying she told me everything, but he was taking too long. I dialed his cell phone. It rang nonstop until the answering machine picked up.

"You have reached Rasheed Williams at Brothers' Enterprises. I'm not available at this very moment, so leave your name and number. I'll get back to you as soon as possible."

I was about to leave a message, but decided against it. I called him again. The phone rang three times before he picked up. "Hello!" He sounded like he was in the club's restroom. I knew exactly where he was at. Music was blasting in the background and his hello echoed. He was at Trey's strip club. I immediately thought of Deanna and came up with a plan.

"Rasheed, where you at?'

"I'm at Stud's studio with Trey. You know, Trey and my nephew been trying to get their own record company started. Especially since Trevon know how to sing."

"Okay, so when are you coming home? You know we rarely even see each other. When I'm at work, you say you at home. And when I'm at home, you say you handling business. Rasheed, there ain't that much business in this world not to spend no time with your wife."

Zena, don't call my phone naggin' me right now. We in the middle of a recording session," Rah said, agitated.

Tears flooded my eyes. "Okay, Rasheed, please just tell me so I can move on with my life. My heart don't lie! I know you are cheating. Just be a man about it. Okay. Rasheed, matter of fact, if you not cheating on me, tell me you love me so I can let you get back to what you were doing."

"Zena, yes I love you. And I'm sorry I'm not home right now. I'm just out handling this bidness. I'm not cheating on you. Just tryna get this money. I'll be home in a few."

"Rasheed, I love you too."

Girl, I Had Enough!

I hung up with Rah feeling at ease with myself. I almost let his charming ways get the best of me once again, but I looked around our big empty house and snapped my fingers. He wasn't slick. I knew he was at Trey's strip club. Sheila had already told me Trey was trying to start his own record company, but didn't have the money because she was slowly fucking him out of a house and home.

I immediately grabbed my car keys and headed out of the door. I was going to teach Rah. He was going to learn one way or the other that he couldn't just run over me and my heart and get away with it. I had my gun and my pocketknife tucked. I didn't know what I was going to do with them, but I felt like Lorena Bobbitt and Zora from the movie Disappearing Acts.

I arrived at the club and observed the scenery before I went in. Fat Pat was not at the front door, so that was a good and bad thing. The bad thing, I couldn't get into the club without being searched. The good thing was, he couldn't give Trey a heads up. I left both weapons in the car and slid some shades and a straw hat on. I knew this would make me look suspicious, but I knew Trey had cameras all around the club. And knowing Trey, he was probably on tactical alert, sitting by one.

I made it to the entrance of the club, hurriedly paid the twenty dollar entrance fee, got patted down, and entered the club with my head down. As I entered the club, Fat Pat walked past me. He did a double take like, damn, I know her. As soon as he snapped his fingers and figured out who I was, he started speed-walking back my way. He called my name "Zena!" But it was too late. I spotted who I was looking for, and my blood pressure shot through the ceiling.

I didn't want to believe my eyes. Rasheed was seated at the bar sipping on a Heineken with Deanna standing between his legs. She had nothing on but some stilettos and a G-string. She kissed him on the lips after he removed the Heineken bottle from them. They were so caught up in their own world, neither one of them saw me coming. Fat Pat was trying his best to catch up to me, but the extra two–to-three hundred

133

pounds he had to carry only allowed him to move so fast.

As I made my way over to the bar, the bartender sat a gin bottle on the counter and ran to the phone. I knew exactly who she was calling. I put a little pep in my step. I then realized the bartender was one of the girls from earlier. What was her name? "Ayana!" She picked up the phone and as soon as she did, I picked up the gin bottle. Before she could say anything, I clubbed Rasheed over the head, splitting everything except the bottle.

Rah fell lifelessly to the floor. I blanked out. I couldn't believe he would go so low. How in the hell could he cheat on me with a stripper? What, my pussy wasn't tight? My asshole wasn't good enough? Even after I thought sodomy was a crime. What, my head was satisfying?

I repeatedly crushed the bottle into Rasheed's head. Blood was everywhere. My heart was racing. Tears were racing down my cheek. And Fat Pat and security were racing over to stop me. I was a possessed woman. I held the bottle tight, looking for Deanna. I wanted her next, but somehow she had vanished.

Fat Pat and his team rushed me from behind. They threw me to the floor. Trey came rushing downstairs. He saw Rah's body laid out and yelled, "Someone call 911!"

Before EMT and LAPD arrived, he called Poppa. Poppa told him let me go. I made it out of the club before the police arrived. I don't know what Poppa told Trey, but when he hung up, he told Fat Pat to get his big ass off of me, and told me to get the hell out of his club . . .

I found myself reminiscing, puffing on my third blunt of kush, sipping my fifth glass of Grey Goose, and now watching Lyfe Jennings's "S.E.X" video. I was bobbing my head, still determined not to cry. I felt since I was stupid enough to accept the nigga back, marry him, and have a daughter by him, I had to suck it up and roll with the punches life was throwing at me.

I replayed Lyfe's video and started singing along with him. "Life's a trip. Heard you just turned seventeen and finally got some hips. Hustlers

Girl, I Had Enough!

on the block go crazy when you lick your lips. But they just want rela-
tions they don't want relationships. Welcome to the real world . . . "

I was determined not to cry, but who was I fooling. As soon as I
got into the song, the floodgates broke. I sobbed like a widow at her
husband's funeral. I was losing my husband, and cherished our vows. It
was to death do us part!

RASHEED

26

After reading Chapter Ten, I called Tiffany the next morning. Momma was in the kitchen cooking breakfast when I leapt up and grabbed the phone. "Boy, at least go wash your face and brush your teeth," she scolded. "Don't think 'cause you grown, you can't get it. I just got on your nephew about getting up and coming straight into the kitchen. And I think the boy's best friend is them goddang headphones. He ain't took 'em off since he been here. He even sleep with 'em. I call his name a hundred times and he say 'huh' like he's deaf. He lowers the volume and still keep 'em on…"

I knew Momma was 'bout to go on and on, so I excused myself and went and did as told. After I finished, I went into the den, away from Momma and called Tiffany. I loved Momma with all my heart, but if you let her, she would have talked your ears off from sun up to sun down. That was probably one of the reasons CJ kept his headphones on.

Tiffany answered on the third ring. "Hello!"

"Good morning, young lady. Did I wake you?"

"In a way yes. In a way no."

"Do you know who this is?"

She let out a deep breath. "My dream come true."

I smiled. "Well, what's my name?"

"Mr. DG Proper," she said excitedly.

"Well, I was calling to let you know I read Chapter Ten and that you are a hot mess."

"Well, did you like it? Did I word everything right? And did I forget anything?'

"Naw, you hit it right on the nose. You had me smiling from ear to ear."

"Well, when am I going to see you again?" she asked in a flirtatious voice.

I smiled, moved the phone away from my ear, stared at it for a minute, and started bouncing my shoulders up and down like I was the man. "You took the words out of my mouth, sexy. I was 'bout to ask you the same thing."

"Well, what are you doing later?'

"Shit, I was hoping we could get together and hang out."

"That sounds good to me. What you got in mind?'

"Well, since you in Rialto, and I'm in LA, I say we meet at Dave and Buster's. Hang out, play a few games, have a few drinks. What you say? That's a date or what?"

Equipped with a bar, a restaurant, games, and a live band, Dave and Buster's is an adult Chuck E. Cheese. Located in Ontario, California, it was a spot couples twenty-one and over hit. Tiffany agreed. "That's a date." We set the time and hung up. Later that night, we met at Dave and Buster's. We played games, ate, downed a few shots of Hennessy, and enjoyed the company of one another. Around twelve, we left Dave and Buster's for the nearest flea bag. Round 2 of our sexcapade started as soon as we entered the room.

Tiffany moaned all night. "That's right, fuck this pussy." She was fiending for a beat down, and that was what she got.

I roused the next morning from slumber because my cell phone was going off nonstop. The ringtone was Ne-Yo's and Fabulous's single "Make Me Better". It was Zena. I leapt up so fast, I scared the shit out of Tiffany. She held her chest as it was heaving up and down.

Girl, I Had Enough!

"You all right?" I asked in a raspy voice.

She nodded, wiping sleep from her eyes.

"I didn't mean to scare you," I said, sliding on my Evisu Jeans. "That was my wife. I got to go."

Tiffany smacked her lips. "So it's still no strings attached after what we talked about last night?"

I pinched the bridge of my nose and sat at the edge of the bed. Tiffany had tossed the covers back, exposing her naked body. It was flawless. Her perky breasts stood at attention, causing my lips to moisten. As she lifted her legs to exit the bed, she groaned in agony. She reached down toward her crotch and groaned "Whool-wee!"

I arched my brows. "You all right?"

She sat with her foot on the floor and palms at her knees, rocking back and forth and side to side. She was in some pain. I knew what it was from. A snide grin spread across my face.

"Ma, you all right? Let me know something."

"I'm okay,' she confirmed. "My pussy just sore as hell. I just need to use the bathroom right quick. But before you leave, we need to talk."

Tiffany teetered to the bathroom in agony. I watched how she walked. I smiled inwardly. When she made it in the bathroom and shut the door, I started bouncing my shoulders. My male ego was sky high. Once again, I beat it up to where she could barely walk. To be rounding forty, I felt like I was in my prime. They say 30's are the new 20's. I felt twenty-nine.

Tiffany shitted on my parade as soon as she exited the bathroom. "Rasheed, how many condoms did you start off with last night?"

That was a curve ball. I screwed my face "Three. Why?"

"How many have you accounted for?"

I looked down at the three Magnum wrappers on the floor and spotted two used rubbers. I felt the third one still squeezing my dick. "I count three. Why?"

Terry Wroten

I sat with a look of concern on my face. Tiffany tapped her foot impatiently. "Then what's this?" She produced a used condom with the base gone. I undid my jeans and let out a deep breath. The condom broke inside her. She looked at me waiting for an explanation.

"I'm not even going to lie. A nigga was so into what we were doing and your shit is so bomb, I don't know when it broke. Shit, it coulda been when you had me pinned on my back with your hands on my chest and tossing that gorilla up and down on me. Ma, I don't even know."

Tiffany gave me a look that let me know she didn't approve of what happened. I couldn't do nothing about it. Accidents happen. Silence filled the room. The only sound came from the birds and the bees outside. I broke the silence. "So this is it. We just gon' sit here? If so, I'm out. I gotta stop by my brother's to wash up away." I grabbed my belongings off the night stand. I removed a Newport from my half-empty pack and headed for the door.

Using her leg, Tiffany blocked the door. "Most bitches will just let you shit on them, but no, not me." She squinted. "Yesterday, I told you I wanted more than just being a fuck-partner. You agreed. You said you want the same thing I wanted. Now you just gon' stick and move 'cause the woman you said you don't love is calling for you to come home!" She folded her arms across her chest.

"Stop acting like that. Ma, you too fine to be getting all aggressive and agitated. What I said yesterday I meant. My wife and I are cool peoples. I got nothing bad to say about her. She's a good woman, probably nags a lot, but she's the mother of my seed. The only problem we got is that we don't have that spark in our sex life or relationship no more. Ever since she done gained a little weight after having Maryam, she has been insecure. Well, it was way before that, but our sex life is whack . . ."

I paused to take a deep breath. "Now, you are like a breath of fresh air to me. So far we have a lot of good chemistry. Tiff, don't fuck that up with getting all dramatic and shit. My twin already got drama with his

140

Girl, I Had Enough!

wife, and I don't need the bullshit or drama."

"I ain't trying to come off as a drama queen," Tiffany said defensively. "But I am a woman. And we work with feelings, so I've already accepted the fact that you married. I just want my respect when you are with me. Don't just throw me to the left on our time."

I lit a cigarette, took a drag, and casually blew the smoke into the air. "Baby Girl, I feel where you coming from. And I understand that a scorned woman is a deadly woman, so I just want us to have an understanding that my wife comes first before anybody."

Tiffany looked as if I stuck my hand in her chest and snatched out her heart and crushed it, but it wasn't like that. I figured the best way to go about things was through honesty. I was a married man who loved my wife. I just wasn't getting the sexual attention I needed at home. I thought Tiffany was going to break down and throw a tantrum, but to my surprise she stayed solid and held fast.

"It's funny how I was just in your situation: a married woman looking for someone to quench my thirst, because my dick-fiending-ass couldn't get it at home. I had no idea that I was going to meet a man who would eventually pit it on me so decent that my marriage would eventually end over him."

I furrowed my brows trying to figure out what she was hinting at.

"Yes. Rasheed, I'm talking about you. The night we did our thing, you showed me what I was missing. Even though my husband had a good job and stability, you released the beast in me. Rasheed, ever since that night, I knew me and my husband wasn't going to last. A year later, we split . . ."

Tiffany went on to say, "This might drive me crazy, but one thing I know fa sho', I'm sticking around. Life is a vicious cycle. And breaking it is the hardest thing to do. It's like they say, 'history repeats itself'. I give you and your wife a year at the most."

I didn't know what to think or say. That was too blunt and bold for my taste. Shit, I couldn't tell if she was a fatal attraction or if it was the way I put it down. I toyed with the thought for a minute and figured it was my dick game. At the end of the day it is proper, I thought.

The best way to deactivate the situation was to relieve some tension. I groped Tiffany's ass and gently ran my tongue down and around her neck. "Baby Girl, check out time ain't until twelve. Why don't you just relax and let Mr. DickGameProper work some tension outta you."

Tiffany smiled. She was a freak. Better yet, nymph. DickGameProper was too. Round 3 on me . . . .

TIFFANY

<u>27</u>

When I made it home, I couldn't stop smiling. After the night and morning with Rasheed, I felt like a new woman. I had finally got what I wanted after two long-long years. I didn't want to admit it, but Rah had me. I was sprung. Not only was his dick the best I'd ever had, but when I found that busted condom in me, I was happy. I felt when it popped. I was on top of him riding his dick like a jockey at the Kentucky Derby. I was working my inner walls. I was giving him my all. I knew his raincoat was open. I rode him until I felt him explode inside of me. I moaned, "That's right, fuck this pussy." And that was exactly what he did.

Round 3, we had no protection at all. My pussy was still sore from the first and second round knockouts, but I had to redeem myself and win my prize trophy. After Rah thought he was going to diss me and throw his wife in my face after he fucked the shit out of my pussy, I wanted to teach him by hook or crook, you play with pussy, you get fucked.

I immediately took his dick into my mouth. I licked around his balls and the inner part of his thigh while stroking his dick and teasing it at the same time. I did this while his nut was building. When I felt he was about to explode, I pushed him onto the bed and straddled him. I rode him nonstop, taking every inch of his dick until he started twitching and trying to throw me off of him. I pinned him down with all my weight and hands on his chest. He was trying to fight it, but I flexed my inner muscles and lowered my face to his earlobe while still slamming my pussy onto his dick.

I held him around the neck and moaned, "Cum on, baby, nut for me. This pussy all yours. Fuck it, baby. Fuck it."

After Rasheed exploded inside me, he buried his face between my legs. How he was eating me out, I took it, he was trying to suck all of his fluids out of me. He licked my pussy from one end to the next. My juices were oozing all over his face. His tongue fucked my vaginal canal in and out, in and out like it was a two-inch dick. I was going crazy. I'd never experienced such pleasure. He ate my pussy savagely, and it was the best I'd ever had.

After all was said and done, Rasheed grabbed his stuff, kissed me on the forehead, and left. It was check out time when he rolled out, but I was too tired and still in Pleasureville to follow his lead. I laid in bed with my legs spread-eagle and my arms stretched outward. I stayed in this position until housekeeping came in and put me out. I drove home on cloud nine. I felt like I hit the jackpot. I just knew I was impregnated.

After I got home and settled down, I hopped in the tub and soaked. I had the lights dimmed and jasmine candles lit. I was soaking in Victoria Secret's strawberry bubble bath. I relaxed and found myself in deep thought. I thought back to when I was a young girl and how badly I wanted to just please my husband, but he turned out to be counterfeit. He showered me with material things and I fell for his trap. But like they say, "money can't buy love".

I sat in the tub and couldn't get my mind off of Rasheed. I was the mistress I wasn't suppose to fall do deep in love. *Am I in love? Or is it the dick?* I asked myself. I dwelled on the two questions for hours. I couldn't come up with an answer. Rah had me going crazy. I was literally losing my mind. I was confused. I didn't know what to expect. It was mind-blowing how one man could just sweep me off my feet.

Girl, I Had Enough!

But, then, what was I doing? He was already taken. He had a family. He had a wife. I couldn't be nothing more than a mistress. The other woman. The woman in the closet. The best thing to do was to fall back and let things play out how they played. I decided to go add to my follow up. The saga continues . . . .

RASHEED

28

Zena sat on the love seat, sipping on some Grey Goose and watching On Demand videos when I walked into the house. She was bobbing her head to Lyfe Jennings's "S.E.X." video. Zena only drank liquor when she was stressed. I smelled the underlining of purple kush, but jasmine filled the air. Zena had her hair wrapped in a bun. Her hazel eyes were greenish-brown, so I knew I was in for a verbal lashing. A lashing that I knew would last for weeks on out.

"Oh, so you finally decided to bring your black ass home?"

She pulled on the blunt dangling from between her lips. "Where you been, Rasheed? I been calling your phone all night and all morning!"

I let out a deep breath. This was the headache that came with running game. You had to keep up will all your lies. "Damn, Zena, I told you I was going to be out all night helping Trey with his record company. You know that nigga is old-fashioned and don't know shit about computers."

Zena held her hand up, like stop the press. "Rah, please, don't lie to me," she said scornfully. "You know that's the same fuckin' lie you used when I caught you cheatin' on me with that stripper bitch. What, you in love with a stripper? Let me know."

"Zena, you trippin again. You letting your insecurities get the best of you."

"Muhfucka, you better stop playin' with me!" she said, agitated. "I give you my all, and in return, you give me bullshit and lies. Rasheed, why you just can't tell the truth? Why you just got to run over me all the goddamn time? Why?"

Zena was on to something. I knew it, but I had to stick to the script. Like old girl said in that magazine, "confessions are for Usher". Oh, and my stupid-ass twin. I pondered the questions and how I was going to tell her the truth - that we were lacking in bed — and I had ventured elsewhere, but, at the same time, I wasn't stupid. There was only one way to answer these questions.

"Zena, what are you talking about?"

I played dumbfounded and even tried to place the guilt trip on her. "Every time a nigga step foot out of this house, it's something. Why you give a nigga another chance, if every time you call and I don't answer, 'cause I'm busy, you think a nigga is fuckin cheatin'?"

She sobbed, "Rasheed, I don't believe you. I accepted your apologies, gave you another chance, and you played me again!"

I didn't like where the conversation was going. I started thinking of all the possibilities and what she could know. My heartbeat quickened, but I held fast. I couldn't let my face reveal what I was really thinking. "Zena, look, you drunk, high, tipsy and trippin' for nothing. I don't know what's your problem, but I'm 'bout to shake this spot until you calm down. I mean, whatta fuck are you trippin' for? Is it cuz I stayed out all night? Let me know something, 'cause I'm starting to think you losing your mind."

Zena snapped. She leapt up from the love seat so fast she nearly fell. From behind her back she pulled out some papers. For a minute, I thought they were some paternity papers or something of that nature. I thought someone was trying to put a baby on me. She threw the papers at me. They fell to the floor. "Look at them and tell me what's that all about."

Girl, I Had Enough!

I bent slowly and picked up the papers. The whole time I kept my eyes on Zena. She was deadly. I smiled, looking at the papers. They were printouts of my Crackbook page and a few of my blogs. I felt a little more at ease. My situation wasn't as bad as I thought. I knew it was only a matter of time before Jada ran her big mouth, because the bitch wasn't getting a dime out of me. I wasn't going to let her con me for money to keep her mouth shut. Stupid is as stupid does. Knowing her triflin' ass, she would have got the money and still ran her mouth. I did some stupid things in life, but I wasn't that stupid.

I laughed. "Zena, I don't believe you trippin' off this bullshit. This ain't nothing but fun and games on the Internet. What's wrong with clowning around on the computer?"

"Rasheed, I don't see what's so fuckin' funny."

Zena was now in my face. At times, it was a turn-on to see her mad. She stood five-foot-two and had an hourglass figure. It was little flabby from giving birth, but it was all right. She looked me in the eyes.

"Rasheed, what's so fuckin' funny?" she fumed. I eased some tension with my laughter. She was expecting a guilty expression and explanation, but I laughed.

"Well, if this will calm you down," I said sarcastically, "the reason I'm laughing is because I don't believe you trippin' off this. Shit, if I thought it was a problem, I wouldn't have joined the shit. Don't you and your sister got a page? Shit, she was the one who put me up on the site. Zena, honestly speaking, I never thought you'd trip."

I tried to sound real sincere, but Zena wasn't buying it. She twisted her lips. "Do you expect me to really believe that?"

"Shit, it's the truth."

"Well, Rah, if it's the truth, and ain't nothing but a little innocent computer game, why in the hell you got a picture on there like you a porno star and going by the name DickGameProper?"

149

Terry Wroten

I doubled over in laughter. "Baby, that's why I love you. You can be so silly at times. But to answer your question, that picture and that name is up there cuz I lost a bet to Calvin and I had to post that picture and that name for three months on my page. I just never changed it."

Zena knew I was full of shit. She shook her head like "yeah right". Then, she started mushing me in the forehead with her index finger. "I'ma make this real clear. Rasheed, I love you, but you walking on thin ice. My heart can only take so much. I always tell you, a scorned woman is very dangerous and deadly."

Zena pulled a .50 Cal Desert Eagle from behind her back. She pointed the gun directly at my forehead. I told myself, This bitch done gone crazy. I had never seen a .50 Cal until this day, but heard all about them. Zena's eyes took on a funny glare. I was scheming on snatching the gun.

"I can read your mind. You try to snatch this gun, one of us gon' die."

"Whoa-whoa-whoa." It finally sunk into my head. This bitch had a gun pointed directly at the temple. I wanted to slap the shit out of her, but I knew not to test Zena. I said, "Man, whattha hell is wrong with you?"

"What's wrong with me is you! You running over me like I'm just some tramp on the street. So hear me out and make sure you understand me clearly, 'cause you ain't gon run over my heart again and get away with it . . ."

"Zena, just speak your mind, 'cause you playing with guns ain't cool."

"And you playing with my heart ain't cool."

"Come on, baby, you trippin' again."

SMACK!

Zena slapped the shit out of me. I couldn't do nothing. I couldn't even tell her to keep her hands to herself. The woman was possessed, and I knew she would've pulled the trigger if I would have made any sudden moves.

Girl, I Had Enough!

She cracked a one-sided smile. "I'm not trippin'? This shit is like déjà vu. I felt this same way when you cheated on me with that stripper. My heart tells me. Believe it or not, most women can feel when their man is cheating on them, and Rah, straight up, I know you are being unfaithful and committing adultery. All I ask is that you don't let me catch you. 'Cause if you do, I'ma put so much lead in you that they gon' need a metal detector to find you."

"Zena, don't threaten me," I shot.

"That's not a threat. That's a promise," she shot back. She gave me the evil eye, lowered the gun, and walked back to the love seat to enjoy the rest of her booze and marijuana. I wanted to rush her from behind and knock her the fuck out, but I decided against it. I just told myself, Boy, you playing with fire. Best tighten ya game up. I walked to the bedroom and slammed the door. I made sure it was locked before I fell asleep. I was tired.

151

TREY

<u>29</u>

Riiiiinnng!
Riiiiinnng!

Candy had been blowing my cell phone up all morning. We'd been messing around for three-and-a-half months. Ever since she put it on me in my office, I couldn't resist the temptation of sticking my dick in her virgin-tight pussy. I thought I was crazy when I came to the conclusion that the more I fucked her, the tighter her pussy seemed to get. She had that snap-back fa sho', but it was more of snap-back-and-get-tighter. Plus, what she did with her mouth, she was knocking all other bitches out of the box. In addition to that, sodomy wasn't a crime with her. She took it in the ass and backed it up at the same time. She was doing the most to only be eighteen. For lack of definition, I felt like T-Pain - I was sprung and in love with a stripper.

My phone rang nonstop. I wanted to answer it, but Candy knew that when I was at home with my wife, she was not to call. I let the phone ring. Sheila looked at me and frowned. She was braiding my hair to the back in zigzag cornrows. I usually kept it pressed straight down, but my son, Trevon, told me I be embarrassing him with my perm and pimpish attire/ways. I decided to get hip, especially since I was meeting with a younger girl. I'd even let Trevon use my credit card to go shopping for me. I was going to be hanging with him for a few weeks, so I let him go to DEMO's, Men's Land, and Up Against The Wall to get me the latest fashion.

Sheila yanked my hair as she braided and said, "Muthafucka, I ain't stupid," agitatedly. "Answer your goddamn phone or turn it off! I know it's one of them mud ducks from the club. I'm telling you, Trey, if you bring home anything, you gon' wish you hadn't. I know you going to be a man, and men cheat. Just do us a favor and keep your shit tight."

I wholeheartedly felt where Sheila was coming from. My wife was one of a kind, but I was a nigga. And a nigga just don't give himself up that easy. I lied, "Woman, hush. Ain't nobody cheating on you. You just want something to talk about. You know that's Momma, and she been calling for me to stop by and talk to CJ er' day, because Calvin gon' kill 'em if he got to sit down and talk to him. Plus, he can't even see his kids right now until that bitch take that goddamn restraining order off him . . ."

Sheila yanked my hair again. "Don't talk about my friend like that. I know she's wrong as two left shoes for putting those kids in their mess, but Calvin's old cheating ass deserves everything he get and got coming…"

"Hol' up, swoll up. That's my little brother you talking about," I warned.

"And if I didn't know that, I'd be one stupid muhfucka. Shit, it run in y'all family to cheat. I wouldn't be surprised if y'all share the ho's y'all cheat with…"

"Ma, is you done yet?" Trevon Jr. asked, stepping out of the kitchen. I was saved by the bell.

"Yeah, I got this last braid and you and your cheatin'-ass father can get the hell outta my house."

I glanced over my shoulder. I was seated on the living room floor between Sheila's legs as she sat on the couch. "Woman, how you gon' put me and my son out of a house I bought?"

Girl, I Had Enough!

Sheila playfully slapped the back of my head. "Boy, will you turn around, so I could knock this last braid out. And to answer your question of how I could put you out... Well, when you bought this house, you was hustling and I was the only one with a job. And I thought I'd give you this fair warning: if you slip up and bring some bullshit home, I'ma show you whose house this is."

I waved Sheila off. "Aw, woman, what's with you and this cheatin' shit lately?"

"First of all, I been fiending for some double fudge cake lately, so someone is pregnant. And I know it ain't Trevona, because she's more worried about school and her books than a nigga. Plus, by the way your cell phone been going off lately, I just feel it."

I dismissed Sheila. I stood up after she finished the last braid. She hooked me up. I turned to her. "Now, how much do I owe you?"

She squinted. "You owe me your life and my life back if I find out you got somebody pregnant."

"Now, Sheila, you know the only person pregnant is that bitch you sit up and talk to all damn day and night, on the phone with. What, she's six or seven months now?"

Sheila snapped her neck from side to side. "For your information, Alice is eight months now. And her baby daddy treat her better than Calvin's no-good-ass."

I chuckled. "How in the hell could he treat her better than Calvin when they both living off Calvin and staying in Calvin's house?'

Sheila cracked a half-smile. "Humph!"

Trevon looked at me and said, "Dad, would you come on! Didn't you say Stud said he 'don't got all day'? Plus, nobody want to hear you and mom bicker all the damn time."

Sheila frowned. "Nigga, I don't care how old you are, you better respect me and watch who the hell you talking to."

I nodded in agreement. "Yep. That's one thing you best always remember."

Trevon nodded. We headed for the door. He said, "I apologize Ma. You know, I love you."

Sheila waved him off. "Well, start acting like it. Don't do me like your father be doing me."

I grunted. "Humph! Shit, I'm always the bad guy."

Trevon said, "Anyway, if a girl named Amiri call, could you tell her I'm out handling bidness? And if Andrea calls, I'm at the studio."

Sheila dismissed us. "Yeah. I'ma do it this time, but you better stop playing with these girls' feelings. One of 'em going to do you like Zena did Rasheed!"

As soon as I got in the car, my cell phone started going off again. It was like Candy just knew I was getting in the car. I answered on the third ring as I backed out of the driveway. "Hello!"

"Dolla, where you at?"

Dolla was my street name. "I'm just now pulling out my driveway. Why?"

"Because we got to talk. And, baby, I need some money."

"Candy, I just gave you some money two days ago. But, look, I got my son in the car with me right now. We 'bout to stop by my mom's house then head to Stud's studio. You could meet me there in a few hours."

"Okay. But first tell me you love me."

"Candy, please, don't put me on blast in front on my son. I told you, he's in the car with me."

Even though Trevon was in his own world typing away on his laptop computer, I wasn't too fond of talking to Candy while he was in my presence. I mean, I was married to his mother. He knew what was going on, but I didn't want to make it seem like my love for Shelia was gone. I loved my wife, but I also loved to test the market and play in the field of unfaithfulness.

Girl, I Had Enough!

Candy said, "Okay. I respect that. But when we are alone, you going yo pay, because I want you to assure me that you love me."

"I do! Just meet me at the studio, and I'll show you.

I hung up with Candy after we said our goodbyes. I looked over at Trevon and he was typing away. I wondered what the hell he was typing? As soon as I was about to open my mouth to ask him, he said, "Dad, I have a question."

I replied, "Shoot."

"Is it me? Or do Momma like to male bash? It seems like she always got something bad to say about men. Will Smith win an Oscar. It's, 'oh that's luck'. Halle Berry win an Oscar and it's, 'go, girl'. And the funny thing, Halle fucked a white man to get it. Michael Vick goes to jail. It's 'that's what he get.' Hillary versus Obama. She's going with Hillary because she's a woman. But goddammit, Obama is black!"

I cracked up laughing. My son was known to spit a few jokes here and there. When he was younger, I took him to the LA Comedy store for junior night. He won three out of five shows. I figured him to be the next Martin Lawrence, but 'bout time he turned fifteen, he and a few of his friends formed a boy-band. They thought they were Dru Hill, but the only person who could sing was Trevon. He was the Sisqo of the group. He ended up falling in love with singing. He called himself "Trey Love".

I laughed until we pulled into Momma's driveway. Before I got out, I told him, "Yes. Your moms has issues with men. She believes we're all dogs. Before I met her, back in college, her first two boyfriends did her wrong. She's been scorned ever since. At one point in time, the whole school thought she was lesbian, especially my old buddy Sam Baker. That is, until she got pregnant with your sister."

I looked at Trevon and he was back caught up in cyberspace. I felt like I was being ignored. I left the topic alone and left him sitting in the car.

Terry Wroten

Momma was sitting at the kitchen table sipping on some Folgers and watching re-runs of *Heat of the Night*. I specifically bought the TV so she could sit and watch it from the kitchen table. The kitchen was like her sanctum. I placed the TV on the counter, and it's been her best friend for the last twenty-one years.

I kissed her on the cheek and took a seat at the table. "Where's Poppa and my hard-headed nephew?" I asked, grabbing an orange from the fruit basket positioned in the middle of the table.

"Well, you know, Poppa ain't doing too well again. He been bed-ridden for the last three days. Think he's coming down with a cold..." Momma paused. Her demeanor went from somewhat up-tempo to sad. Tears rushed to her eyes. "But who I'm worried about is that goddang Calvin Junior. It seems like my cries falls on deaf ears. I been telling you and your brother to talk to the boy for the last two months. Y'all ain't gon' be happy until that poor boy gets killed. Even Melvin stopped by after doing all that time in prison with Byrd. They came to see Poppa, but Melvin spent a good hour trying to talk some sense into that boy's head. He did good for two days, then he was back coming home high, drunk, and with his pants so low you could see his two-way."

Tears rushed to Momma's eyes. I immediately fumed. Since I was a child, I'd always been over-protective and a momma's boy. I felt like breaking my nephew's jaw. As soon as I was about to ask "where he at?" he came strolling through the door, pants below his waist. He was sagging so hard, he could barely walk. He had a Discman in his hand and his headphones were at top volume. He was bobbing his head to Young Jeezy's single "Trapstar". He was draped in blue everything. He even had a blue bandana hanging from his Levis rear left pocket. I had heard he was a Crip, but now I knew he was a Crip. There was no ifs, ands, buts about it. He was bangin'.

I shook my head at him. He knew nothing about Crippin', yet, he had a mob that was out of this world. You would have thought he was

158

Girl, I Had Enough!

Nino Brown, John Gotti or somebody. But I knew the real! He was just a teen at the peak of an identity crisis. I had to break him from his misdirection. And by the way he was hurting my momma, I wanted to choke him out.

"What up, Unc, Cuzz?' he greeted in a mock-gangster tone of voice while reaching out to hug me.

I was not feeling little dude. Even though, he was the size of Fat Pat, I wanted to take him down. I couldn't stand to see my flesh and blood caught up in a life he knew none to little about. He wasn't brought up in the streets. Calvin had literally pampered this boy until he was fifteen. That was the reason he was the biggest dude in the family. Calvin spoiled him and didn't realize that the drama he and Alice were going through was affecting their kids the most.

CJ reeked of weed and Hennessy. I pushed him off of me. "Fool, I ain't yo' homeboy. Get off me!" I snapped.

I stood up. We stood face to face. He was three inches taller than me and had me by a hundred and twenty pounds. I gave him the evil eye and a one-sided smile. I wanted him to flinch or do something. I was going to put him on his back.

Just as I was about to chin-check him and bring him down a few levels, Momma stood up and got between us. "Trevon, I didn't say hurt the boy. I said talk to him."

"Momma, nowadays, you can't talk to these kids, you got to put a foot up their behind."

Momma agreed. "Yeah, I know, but just try to talk to him. I don't want you doing none of that karate stuff on him. I don't want you to go to jail. I'm already stressing over his father."

I was a third-degree black belt. I had to register my hands and feet as deadly once a year. Momma knew if I laid a finger on CJ, I was going to jail. I backpedaled with my fist still balled. The funny thing is, I glanced CJ in the eyes and realized he was so intoxicated he didn't even know what was going on, and his headphones were still at top volume around his ears. The nigga didn't hear shit I said.

I fumed. Before I knew it, I snapped. I slapped the Discman out of his hand. It fell to the floor and Young Jeezy's Thug Motivation CD popped out. All in one motion, I grabbed him by the neck like the Undertaker and spat, "Look here, nigga, I'll be a rat's ass if I stand here and let yo' big ass walk in this house high as a kite, pants below your waist, and blue rag hanging from your back pocket. Young street punk, you know nothing about being a Crip. You ain't a Crip. I will break your fuckin' jaw. You hear?"

CJ gasped for air. "Ye-yes." I had a lock on his jugular that let him know I was as serious as AIDS in Africa. This was no joking matter to me. His high instantly came down. Tears filled his eyes. He knew I was a master in the art of fighting. Momma had trophies all over the house. Pictures of me at different tournaments lined the walls. He knew I could have killed him if that was what I wanted. But all I wanted him to know was he had to respect somebody.

Momma grabbed my arm. "Okay, Trevon, that's enough. You gon' kill the boy."

I released my grip. I was so mad, I started pacing in front of CJ, hoping he would say or do something. LA was gang heavy and the Crips and Bloods were really doing their thing, but nothing like when I was growing up. I figured if I grew up in the late 70's and 80's when the Crips and Bloods were really doing their thing, and nI had ever joined, why should I settle for my nephew claiming Crips while living in my parents' house?

"Nigga, at least move out, get your own shit, and then gang bang. Which is something I don't want you to do. But don't gang bang while living with my parents, your grandparents, and get this house shot up."

I ended up talking to CJ for three hours straight. The funny thing is, my son stayed in the car on that computer the whole time. I felt I needed to show CJ some tough love. After I seen he was not as gangsta as he was portraying, I loosened up. I just wanted to break him down and let

Girl, I Had Enough!

him know what he was involving himself with. Plus, from my knowledge of the streets I knew he wasn't a true hardcore gang member. A true gangster at heart would have tried to take my head off (uncle or not)! And that's with fist or gun. The Crips motto is: Can't stop. Won't stop. Will not be stopped. So I knew if CJ let me stunt on him like I did, he was not as gangsta as he fronted.

I patted my nephew on the back to ease some tension. I was his uncle. I didn't want him to start resenting me. I didn't want him to hate me. I had to explain why I did what I did, and let him know it was only 'cause I loved him and what he was doing was wrong.

"CJ, it's more to life than gang bangin'. Hanging in the hood, on the block, getting drunk and high ain't shit. It's for two people and two people only: jail birds and walking corpses. CJ, you are hurting everybody in the family. You hurting your granny. Look at her! You hurting your father the most. He's trying his best not to flip on you 'cause of what he's going through. And you hurting me. You my favorite nephew. I don't wanna see you go out backwards or in a grave. Why don't you go to school and play ball? I'll pay for it. Or shit, just tell me what you like to do that's positive, and I'll pay for it."

"I'm not too good at football, but I know how to sing."

I cracked a one-sided smile. I thought, *Do this nigga really know how to sing?* I said, "All right. Let me hear something."

CJ hit a few verses for me. Come to find out the boy could really sing. He had talent. I figured it ran in the family. He sang three songs that he wrote, and brought Momma to tears. She was proud of him for the very first time in a long time. Momma was an alto back in her younger days, and she knew talent when she saw it.

She kissed CJ on the cheek. "Now, that's the grandson I know. Boy, you sound great. Just a little practice and you'll be all right."

CJ had one song in particular that fit him to a T and stood out the most. It was called "Teddy Bear". It went something like this:

161

Terry Wroten

"Teddy-Teddy-Teddy-Teddy Bear/Teddy-Teddy-Teddy-Teddy Bear/ That's me ...

That was the hook. The song was a hit. It started off with the hook and repeated itself twice. Then, CJ crooned some lyrics about how he was soft and cuddly and wanted a girl to come cuddle with him. The song was nice. CJ reminded me of American Idol winner Ruben Studdard. I had to get him in the studio with Trevon FAST! They were a perfect match and very talented.

"Have you ever been to a studio?"

CJ nodded his head. "Yep. I be in the studio er' day. I probably be faded, but I don't be hanging out how y'all think. My boy, Gully, got this own studio in his room. It's probably the ghettoest studio you'll ever see, but it's where we record. It's four of us right now. Me, Gully, Smacka, and Bump Johnson. I'm the only singa. Well, I could do both. I'm like a rappa turned singa."

I was surprised. Just like always, there was more to a young black man when you look inside him. My nephew was multi-talented and had already formed a crew. That was very impressive. His situation wasn't as bad as I thought it was. Like they say, "never judge a book by its cover". All CJ needed was some tough love and strong guidance. He was a star in the making. A diamond in the dirt. I was on to something new.

"All right, look, tonight you hanging out with me and Trevon. Matter of fact, go tell that Negro to get off that computer and come speak to his grandma, so we can roll to this studio and let y'all record some stuff."

CJ nodded and walked off. As soon as he slammed the door, my cell phone went off. For a minute, I thought it was Candy, but looking at the Caller ID, it was KC. What she want? If it ain't one thing, it's another, I thought.

I answered on the second ring. "Hello!"

SHEILA

<u>30</u>

"Well, what's good for the nigga is better for the bitch," I told KC as we sat in the living room of the house. She pulled up a few minutes after Trey and Trevon left. She was telling me that word around Red Light District was that a young stripper called Candy was supposedly pregnant by Trey. My initial response was, "Bitch, I felt it." The funny thing is, KC had brought Candy home one night, and we all indulged in a threesome. I buried my face between Candy's legs and tasted her creamy cum as I licked and slurped her pussy from one end to the next. Her juices were oozing all over the mattress. I tongue-fucked her until she begged KC to fuck the lining out her pussy with the 10-inch strap-on.

While KC pounded her pussy missionary style, I sat on her face. She moaned and groaned from the pleasure she was receiving from KC, but she still managed to suck my pussy until I nutted. Then, while KC rammed the strap-on inside of me, Candy massaged and sucked my breasts. We freaked each other all night, and KC even had a camera hidden in the closet for her own personal satisfaction.

But like I was saying. "Girl, I'm telling you, I felt it. I even told the nigga earlier that somebody was pregnant. You know when I be fiending for some double fudge cake it never fail, but for a minute, I thought it could be Trevon's ass. You know, he's just like every dog on his dad's side of the family . . ."

Riiiiinnng!

Riiiiinnng!

"Matter of fact, hol' on, this might be for his young dog-ass now." I picked up the cordless phone and answered on the second ring. "Hello!"

"Hello! Hi! Is Trevon home?"

"May I ask who's calling?"

"Amiri."

I wanted to say, "Amiri, Trevon, doesn't live here. He has his own house. He stays with his girlfriend. Her name is Andrea. They stay in Lawndale. And the number is . . ."

However, I simply told her what Trevon told me to tell her. "Amiri, Trevon is not home right now, but he left a message for you. He told me to tell you he's out handling business with his father, and he'll call you as soon as he gets back in."

Amiri said, "Okay. Thank you," and hung up.

I turned back to KC. "Anyway. Like I was saying. I knew somebody was pregnant. I just didn't think it'd be the young bitch we fucked. It's okay though, because now I got a reason to do what I'd been waiting to do. I can finally come out of the closet and move to Atlanta like we been talking about, with a pocket full of money. Like I said, what's good for the nigga is better for the bitch. You play with pussy, you get fucked!" A snide grin spread across my face.

KC crossed her ankles. "Baby, what yo' triflin' ass plotting now?"

"I might be evil-minded and vengeful, but never triflin'." I rubbed by palms together; they had begun to sweat. I loved Trey. He, Trevon, and Poppa were the only men in my life who held a piece of my heart. My father had died a few years back, so these were the only men I cared for. I cared for my husband so much; I could have pulled one of Alice's stunts. He cheated on me so much, I could've burnt down the house, filed for divorce, and slept with other men and tossed them in his face. I even could have gone out of my way to bruise my body and call 911.

Girl, I Had Enough!

His hands were deadly and had to be registered every year, so he would've been facing or doing a nice bid in state prison. But I cared for Trey too much to ever put him through such heartache, headache, and pain. I knew what he was doing. All I asked was he take care of home and make sure his cheating games stayed between him and whoever he was fucking, but since he couldn't, it was going to cost him. I was tired of his shit and he was going to pay.

"Well, since he like young pussy, I'ma let him have her. Me and you 'bout to get all our shit and head to the south. Where you want to go, South Beach or Hot-lanta?"

KC cracked a half-smile. "Shit, either one of them is a go."

"All right. This what I need you to do. I need you to call Trey and ask him if he is coming in tonight. He keeps his bank cards and statements all in one of those file cabinets in y'all office. He keep 'em locked, but he leave the spare keys in his bottom drawer in our room. I need to make copies of the statements and steal them cards. I also need you to some-how pull out. Tell him you 'bout to move out of state somewhere. I'ma put the house on the market first thing in the morning."

KC playfully pinched my cheeks and smiled. "That's what I'm talk-ing about, baby. Now, I finally get to have you all for myself after all these years." She gently kissed me on the lips and groped my breasts. Then, she stuck her tongue down my throat. I became moist between the legs. Before I knew it, she was on top of me with her hands inside my pants, twirling her fingers in and out my soaked pussy. The cum between my legs felt like glue. I could feel my clit jump up and down with joy as KC kept hitting my G-spot. However, we had bigger fish to fry. It was business before pleasure.

Betweens breaths of air, I moaned, "Baby, wait. Hold on. Call Trey first, so we can get him out of the way."

KC immediately did as told. She grabbed her cell phone and dialed Treys' phone. He answered on the second ring. I noticed he had never answered my calls on the second ring. It was more on the second call or not at all. It was funny how men acted as if they don't know it's the small things that get them caught. I just laughed to myself as KC talked to him on the other end of the phone. It was like women normally got smacked with the dick, rather than fucked with it. But I told myself, "Never again!"

KC hung up with Trey and turned to me, smiling from ear to ear. "That nigga said he gon' be at the studio all night with Trevon and CJ. We got all night to fuck and do what we gotta do."

TREY

31

"If you know like I know nigga stack ya chips / If you know like I know nigga stack ya chips / I put that on Foety Third / I put that on Foety Third / Yeah my name Scatter Brain niggas / Better known as Dat Nigga Big Stud Loc / You see me in the hood I'm steady gettin' bigga / You didn't know you betta ask somebody / Born and raised doing this Crip shit / Use to call me Kill Rat until Killa Black told me to switch the script and stack / So if you know like I know nigga stack ya chips . . . "

Stud's studio was crowded when CJ, Trevon, and I arrived. Stud was in the booth smoking a blunt and going crazy on a track. Stud was a famed underground rapper out of LA who started out as a Crip under a legendary Crip called Killa Black. Killa Black was a Crip who every Crip in South Central respected. Stud was Killa Black's protégé. Stud went by a different name back then, but a lot of people knew about his street credibility. He was a cold-blooded youngster growing up. When he started rapping, he was already known, and everything he rapped about, people felt and knew he was speaking the real.

Groupies filled the garage-turned-studio like it was a club. Stud was most known for his songs "50 Niggas Deep", "Evil Side", and "Free Dee Bast". He was also known for working with a lot of industry main-hitters. He was in the stages of developing a few of his own artists: Bossman, Dirty Dee, Toe Tagger, and Murk. These four kids were raw and extremely talented. They had a song called "Deep Throat" that was getting rotation up and down the California coast. I'd met Stud at a mansion party a few years back. He had come to the club passing out flyers, so I decided to go. I brought Diamond, Ayana, and a few other dancers along with me. They ended up turning the party out. Stud and I exchanged numbers and had been supportive of each other ever since.

"What it do, folks?" Stud greeted, stepping out of the booth.

We exchanged hand shakes. "Well, I brought my son and nephew to record a few songs with you."

Stud smiled. "Well, who's first?'

CJ stepped into the booth. He recorded "Teddy Bear" first. After the song was over, one of the groupies who was sitting to the side did a double take. "Damn, who is that, Ruben Studdard?"

I smiled. "Naw, ma, Teddy Bear."

She said, "Yeah his big ass could sing."

Stud looked at me and shook his head. "Whoo-wee! Dolla, this boy is vicious."

I nodded in agreement. As I nodded my head my phone went off. I looked at the caller ID. It was Candy. I stepped out the studio and answered, "Hello!"

"Baby, I'm out front. It's the yard with the purple gate and a lot of people out front, right?"

"Yeah. Stay there. I can see you parking right now."

I hung up. I tapped Trevon on the shoulders; he was at the entrance of the studio seated with his laptop in his lap, typing away. I wondered why that boy never gave his computer a break? I was going to find out after I came back from seeing Candy. When my son turned my way, I told him, "I'll be right back; step into the booth after CJ."

He nodded, never looking up from the computer monitor.

I made it up the street to where Candy had parked. She was sitting in her bucket chewing some Big Red and making bubbles. I hopped in the passenger seat and smiled. "What it do, young lady?"

Girl, I Had Enough!

Candy looked good as always. She had on some Seven jeans with matching open-toe heels and a halter top. Her nails were freshly done up with French tips. She had her hair in an Afro ponytail. Her chestnut eyes sparkled and her full lips glistened from the gloss she had on them. Candy was simply beautiful. I pecked her on the lips. I told myself, *Damn, I love this young bitch.*

"Candy, I love you, girl," I said, stroking her chin.

She cocked her neck to the side. "You sure you ain't just saying that?"

"I won't open my mouth, if I gotta lie."

Candy twisted her lips. "Well, I got to tell you something, but I don't know how you gon' take it."

It seemed like everything paused. I ran my hand across my chin and rubbed my eyes. I just felt whatever she was about to tell me had something to do with what Shelia was talking about earlier. My wife's superstitious belief that whenever she fiended for double fudge cake someone was pregnant was accurate as a sniper. It never failed. And I knew exactly what Candy was about to tell me.

I looked at her and said, "Just gon' ahead and get it out."

I was hoping she'd say something different from what I was thinking, but I was up shit's creek.

"Dolla, I'm pregnant!"

I shook my head disbelievingly. I slammed my fist into the dashboard. "Damn!" I yelled. I couldn't even deny it like I wanted to. I couldn't count on my hands how many times I went into Candy unprotected. I slipped up and did what I was telling Rasheed and Calvin not to do. Shelia always told me, "You play with pussy, you get fucked". I couldn't believe I just let myself get caught up. Barry White said it best: "practice what you preach". And I didn't. I was disgusted, disappointed, and pissed all at the same time. How in the hell was I'm going to get out of this?

"Pregnant!" I repeated, trying to get my thoughts together.

Terry Wroten

"Yes. Pregnant. Three months pregnant!"

I felt she had set me up. To me, it was all her fault. "Damn, Candy, how in the hell you fuck around and get pregnant? Man, I told you I got a wife at home. You gots to get an abortion."

Tears rushed to her eyes. She frowned. "I knew you was going to say that. But I refuse to kill another baby. . ."

Come to find out, Candy had been impregnated when she was sixteen, and the father of the child told her to get an abortion. She knew it was wrong, but still did it to satisfy her man. But as time went by, her conscience wouldn't let her sleep. She promised herself if she ever became pregnant again, she would raise the baby alone if she had to.

After Candy cried her heart out, telling me about her story, I thought about how my parents were strictly against abortions. Momma literally forced Charlene to have Charles. Even though I was grown, I knew I couldn't force Candy to have an abortion. I had to slap myself in the face for being so stupid and go to plan B.

"All right, look, first start this car and go to the nearest liquor store. I need the strongest shit they got."

Candy turned the ignition to the car with tears streaming down her face. I reached under her halter top and ran my hand across her belly. I felt the tightness. I kissed her on the cheek. "Don't cry, we gon' get through this."

She put the car in gear and drove off. A few blocks over, we spotted a liquor store called Wine Barrel on 42nd Street and Hoover. Stud studio was on 41st Street and Hoover. A group of winos were sitting outside on crates. I called one to the car as Candy parked.

"Ay, look, run in there and get me a fifth of Jack and some pork rinds. You can have the change." I handed the drunk a twenty and he hurried off. I reclined in my seat and rubbed my forehead. My mind was speeding. I didn't know what to say next. The problem now was that I needed Candy to work with me and keep her pregnancy on the low. I didn't need no one in the club to know. How them bitches gossiped, I knew

Girl, I Had Enough!

word would spread like a transmitted disease and get to Shelia in a flick of a thumb.

"Candy, look ma, I know how you feel. You want to keep the baby, and I gots to respect that, but I need you to be honest. Do you really think it's mine? And have you told anyone in the club that you are pregnant by me?"

Candy nodded, wiping tears from her eyes. "Yes, the baby is yours. You are the only nigga I've been fuckin'. And I told Sinnamon. She went to the doctor with me."

"Damn!" I frowned. I felt like I was living a nightmare and was waiting for someone to wake me up. The wino did just that when he appeared outside the window with the booze and pork rinds. With the quickness, I popped open the Jack Daniels and downed two gulps of the fiery liquor. I let out a deep breath, made a funny face, and wiped my mouth with the back of hand.

Candy turned the ignition and headed back to the studio. She parked in the same spot. We sat in silence while I tilted the bottle. I sat thinking how Sinnamon had the biggest mouth in the club. I felt like beating the baby out of Candy. Even though Sinnamon was her sister and the one who introduced Candy to dancing, it was like, damn, out of all the bitches you could have told, you told the bitch with the biggest mouth. I just knew fa sho' Sheila was going to find out. And by the way she was acting earlier, there was no doubt in my mind that she didn't already know. I decided to play it by ear.

'Bout time the liquor started to kick in, I told myself, Fuck it! Sheila'd understand. She ain't going nowhere. She been with a nigga too long. And we got two kids together.

I glanced over at Candy. She now had her arms on the steering wheel with her face buried between them. I grabbed her by the ponytail and lifted her head up. "Girl, don't never let me see you with your head down. You's a strong woman. We gon' get through this. You might be young, but you know your shit. So check game… From now on, I want

171

you to start stackin' your money. Whatever you make at the club put up, cause it's gon' get hard. Kids cost money, you know? And as long as we keep you away from my wife, we'll be cool. Shit, I'm hoping this record company shit take off so I can get you a new car and a cool place to stay. But, right now, you just need to fall back, all right?"

Candy simply nodded. I didn't know how to take her uneasy demeanor. I kissed her on the forehead and asked, "Are you with me?"

She replied. "Are you the father of my child?"

I faked a smile. "All the time."

She said, "Well, I'm with you all the time."

I gently kissed her one last time on forehead and told her "I love you." She leaned over and stuck her tongue down my throat. "I love you too."

I leapt from the car a little tipsy. I stuck my head back in the car. "I'ma call you later and we gon' get all this shit situated, because when it's said and done, I might have to be living with you in your Section Eight apartment." I was joking, yet serious as a heart attack. I just knew Shelia was going to put my black ass out. Or was it just the liquor talking?

TREY

32

When I stepped back into the studio, CJ and Trevon were in the booth together. They were recording a song called "Better Me" that Trevon had wrote, but needed someone to rap a few verses. CJ took on the job. They recorded "Better Me" over one of Stud's monstrous tracks; Trevon kicked a heartfelt hook and CJ murdered the track. He spat:

"Ma, you gotta go the distance / I need a girl who can carry the weight / I'ma marry her on the first date / Better Me / I'ma better the crew / Better Me / I'ma better you / Teddy Bear that's me / A young black man in this struggle and I'm ready to eat / Better Me…"

I sat in the same seat Trevon sat in before he went into the booth. He lhad eft his laptop in the chair to save his seat. To a lot of folks, the studio was just a hangout (mostly for Stud's entourage). But in the hood, where you got live music, marijuana, a few heads, and booze, you got a party atmosphere. I sat tipsy, bobbing my head to "Better Me". I felt the song. I knew it was a hit. It seemed like CJ's lyrics were right on point with my current situation. I needed Candy to better me by falling back and working with me every step of the way, then I could better her. I sat in my own world with Trevon's laptop resting on my lap, sipping the last of my booze, and bobbing my head to my son's and nephew's song. Even though my situation wasn't looking too good, I was proud of them. *Yeah, niggas make me proud,* I thought. I was clapping drunkenly off-beat, but I couldn't do nothing but be proud. I was helping Trevon and CJ reach their dreams. The funny thing is, the same thing that makes you smile make you cry.

I was hot and cold sitting in that seat. One minute, I was proud of myself for the things I had accomplished. The next, I was mad at myself for the things I'd done. I told myself, *Damn, life has more up and downs then a roller coaster.* Snoop Dogg said it best: "Up and down, smiles and frowns".

"Fuck it, nigga! Stop bitchin' over spilled milk. Life goes on."

After Trevon and CJ recorded "Better Me", Stud called for a weed break. He was producing all the tracks, so we were on his time. He pulled out a dime bag of kush and tossed it Big Wrap. Big Wrap was Stud's road dawg. They were ace coon boons and potheads. Come to find out, everyone in the studio puffed on the blunt a few times. I'd thought my son was a sober body. It fucked me up seeing him puff on the blunt. I had to ask myself, Am I drunk, or did my son just hit the blunt?

Trevon caught my glare. "What's up dad? What's on your mind?"

I chuckled. I was buzzed. "Nigga, did I just see you hit the blunt? Or am I trippin'?"

Stud passed me the blunt after he puffed twice and filled his lungs. He held the potent weed in, then casually blew out the smoke. He yelled "Fiyyah! On the G."

I looked at my son after I puffed on the blunt a few times, intoxicating my lungs. I wasn't an everyday weed smoker, but I did like to get high every now and then. Not to a point where I couldn't make decisions and be all fucked up, but just high enough to feel a buzz and feel good. However, after seeing Candy, I didn't care how buzzed or tipsy I got. I just needed something to escape reality.

Trevon glanced at me and replied, "Yep. I hit the blunt. Since my freshman year of high school." My eyes widened. I thought he was

Girl, I Had Enough!

going to say since his freshman year of college. Then, I realized he followed my lead and was a college dropout after his freshman year. "I started when I first got to Taft. My white friend Mark's parents used to grow the shit and give it to him. We used to ditch school and be at his house, getting high and browsing Myspace."

I didn't know what the hell Myspace was, but kept listening. "This is how I know how to get our music out there. I used to help Mark with his rock band. This is why I've been tellin' you to hurry up and get the company started, 'cause social networking is the shit. Right now it's all about Facebook."

After the short weed break, Stud, his four protégés, and CJ went back into the booth all at once and recorded some tracks together. Trevon grabbed his laptop from my lap, and Big Wrap and I crowded around him. Trevon took his laptop with him everywhere he went. I wondered what he hid in there? Or what was so fuckin' amazing about the thing that he had to have it with him 24/7. For a long time, I thought he was a geek or something. I didn't understand computers at all. I was old-fashioned. I didn't deal with technology. I left that to my brothers. I was lost in time. And as a late 80's baby, I forgot my son represented a generation that doesn't know a world without the world wide web.

However, to my surprise, Big Wrap even knew how to operate a computer, and he was only a year younger than me. So it wasn't just the trend for the younger generation. Technology was in. And I was lost, played out, and tired.

"Damn, Dolla, you don't know what you missin', my nig," Big Wrap informed me. "This technology shit make things ten times easier from when we were comin' up. Take for example cassette tapes and how they played out to CDs. Now, muhfuckas ain't buying CDs. They download-ing songs into their iPod. Companies aren't signing niggas to whole album deals no more. They sign muhfuckas to one-song deals, then put their single out as a ringtone. If that ringtone do good, it cover the cost to drop the album. Look, I got this magazine I want you to check out right quick before your son take you through the journey of Facebook. I'm telling you, with this knowledge I'm 'bout to lace you with, and with your son's genius computer skills, you'll be miles ahead of the game. I be tryna lace Stud, but he's too stubborn and stuck in his own ways when it come to music. He feels he knows everything and don't believe in each one teach one."

Wrap handed me the magazine. It wasn't one that I'd heard of. I even forgot the name after I opened it. Wrap said, "Turn to page fifty-five."

I did as told. I looked at the article. It read:

The Recording Industry Associations of America (RIAA) released a statement that sales of CDs, cassettes, and videos, have fallen 8.9% from last year. With ringtones sales skyrocketing, CDs will soon play out just like cassettes. U.S. ringtone sales totaled $600 million in 2005 and $800 million in 2006. This is according to BMI, which tracks sales data on more than 300 outlets for the sale of mobile entertainment.

Music executives say that ringtones have multiple purposes; you can use them as a marketing tool that will help lift sales of single albums, because they are both a commercial and promotional tool. With increasing sales of nearly 130%, most major companies have established downloadable music videos, albums, and singles. With sales generating billions annually worldwide, newcomers need to immediately jump onto this fad.

I shook my head after closing the magazine. The numbers alone made my palms sweat. I'd always felt the music industry was for me. It was time for me to claim my stake. I was all smiles.

I glanced over at my son on the computer. He was setting up a Facebook page for us. I asked him, "Whatchu doing?"

He simply replied, "Doing a Soulja Boy."

I furrowed by brows. "What the hell is a Soulja Boy?"

Girl, I Had Enough!

Trevon laughed. "Damn, Dad, you need to go check into computer 101 or something. I knew you were lost in time, but I didn't know to this extent . . ."

Come to find out, my son was talking about the young rapper who broke into the music industry by using his Myspace page. I didn't know how the hell Soulja Boy did it, but Trevon explained.

"See, Dad, I can put our music on Youtube and different music sites so people can download our music for free. This way, we create a buzz. But instead of just letting folks download one or two songs, let's put a whole album available for free."

"Also, with a page Facebook, we could connect and start a fan base. This way we could talk to our fans and see what they want to hear and build a fan/artist relationship."

I smiled. Trevon was a business brain just like me. The kid was a genius when it came to computers. I felt good. And I felt that starting this record label was money in the bank.

It was quarter to three when we left the studio. I thanked Stud for his time and headed home. It was too late in the wee hours to drop CJ off at Momma's house, so he went to stay the night at Trevon's. Plus, they planned on working on music together. When I made it home, Sheila's car wasn't in the driveway and the house was so quiet you could hear a rat piss on cotton. *Damn, where this bitch?* I thought. It was Monday and the beginning of a work week, so Shelia would normally be in bed.

I started to panic. Damn, did this bitch find out about Candy and get ghost? Is she out fucking another nigga? Damn, where could she be? I know not at Zena's, because I talked to Rah and he said Zena been trippin' and staying at her sister's lately, getting drunk and high into the wee hours. I know she ain't at Alice's, because her boyfriend ain't been letting her do nothing as of lately, which is a good thing. At least, somebody got that bitch in check. And KC at the club. Well, I'ma give this bitch an hour before I start calling around.

177

Terry Wroten

After I hopped in the shower and lay down, Sheila came tiptoeing through the door. I had the lights off. She thought I was asleep. As she tried to ease in bed, I calmly asked, "And where have you been?"

Caught off guard, she stuttered, "Uh, uh, I was at Zena's house and lost track of time."

She lied and I knew it, but I was glad she wasn't in a shitty mood. That meant she didn't know about Candy like I had thought. Or if she did, she wasn't saying nothing about it. So I decided to leave the subject alone and get a few hours of sleep. I planned on hitting city hall early. I grunted, "Humph!" and fell asleep.

The next morning I arose full of energy and drove down to city hall. Starting a record company and getting it off the ground was all new to me, but I knew with my son's intelligence, work ethic, and net-savvy we were going to make it big. Plus, I was loving the whole vibe of working with Trevon and CJ and helping them develop as artists. I also was going to need the extra income knowing Candy was pregnant, because she was one money-hungry broad. I was content with this new venture. It was exciting and kept my mind off the bullshit yet to come. Reality was that it was only a matter of time before Shelia found out, but, to me, I felt she'd get over it after awhile.

It was a quarter to ten when I made it to city hall. I filled out all the paperwork to get the company started and paid the filing fees. The old white lady who was helping me with the process looked over all the papers to make sure I filled out everything properly. She said, "One last thing. You forgot to put your company name."

That was the problem, I didn't have a company name. I had to think of one real fast. The first thing that came to mind was Dolla Records. I signed Dolla Records on the papers and handed them back to the lady. She looked over them and nodded. "That's a nice name. If it don't make dollars, it don't make sense."

I agreed. "You got that right."

178

Girl, I Had Enough!

She winked and walked off. If I didn't know no better, I would have thought the old white lady was flirting with me. When she returned, she handed me copies of the registration for the company and a receipt.

She smiled. "By the way, are you starting a hip-hop recording company?"

I cracked a one-sided smile. "Sure is."

She said excitedly, "I love hip-hop. Especially Snoop Doggy Dogg."

I wanted to ask the old white what she knew about Snoop Dogg and hip-hop, but decided against it. Hip-hop was the new fad, so her grand kids could have hipped her. I just smiled and walked off.

I exited city hall and was headed to my car when I ran into Rah. This surprised the hell out of me. Rah wasn't a morning person. If he didn't have business to handle, he slept in until the afternoon. Rah was a night crawler. However, what caught my eyes was the beauty he was holding hands with. Rah was living a double life, something I knew nothing about. I knew he cheated from time to time, but I didn't know he was bold enough to be walking in Downtown LA holding his mistress's hand.

His eyes widened seeing me. "Damn, what you doing down here?" he asked as we stood face to face.

"Shit, I should be asking you that," I replied, giving him the look like who is she? "But anyhow, I'm down here because I just registered my record company."

Rah shook his head. He turned to the Halle Berry lookalike and told her he'd meet her at the court, but first he introduced us. "Tiffany, this my older brother, Trey." Tiffany extended her hand. "And Trey this Tiffany. My GIRLFRIEND!"

My eyes widened hearing "girlfriend". Rah was playing with fire. We all were, but he was playing with a powder keg. I waited as Tiffany walked off and asked, "Where you find her?"

"Shit, you want the truth or a lie?"

Terry Wroten

"The truth. muhfucka!"

"Crackbook."

"Nigga, whatta hell is CRACKBOOK!"

I was confused. Come to find out, Rah was talking about Facebook. "Damn, I thought Facebook was for artists to promote and showcase their music."

Rah laughed. I countered "What's so damn funny?"

"Bruh, Crackbook is a site where people log on to chat and meet friends. However, it's so big and has so many members that people go on there to advertise their goods. See, Trey, I told your years ago to get with this technology and get you a computer, but you didn't listen. Now, you don't know shit about it."

I shot back, "Sure don't. But I know one thing, you one crazy nigga walking around in public holding Tiffany's hand. She's a bombshell, but Zena is a time bomb waiting to explode."

Rah waved me off. "Come on, my dude, you know, I got everything under control."

I shook my head shamefully. I couldn't say too much how my situation on was looking, Rah was still my little brother. "Well, I hope you do, cause if you don't it's gon be a cold summer and hot winter for you. I mean, I hope Tiffany is worth it."

Rah pulled out a Newport and lit it. He patted me on the back. "Bruh, believe me, I got this." He walked off.

When I made it to the car, I thought about my situation and how hard it was to resist a beautiful woman, especially a beautiful black woman. Throughout my marriage of twenty odd years, I cheated on my wife a lot. I was no saint, but I did not know what Rah was thinking. He must have forgotten about the psychopath he had as a wife. I did what I did because my wife was more on a dog going to be a dog, just don't bring none on my bones home. He had more to lose. His wife was fatal!

I drove all the way from city hall to Red Light District, which was a thirty or forty minute drive on the street, thinking about Rah. For some

Girl, I Had Enough!

reason, I felt his situation was more of importance than mine. I knew it was none of my business, but I couldn't help but think about the time Zena caught him cheating and damn near killed him. Somehow, she got word that Rah was dating one of the dancers who worked at my first club named Deanna. She disguised herself and got into the club unnoticed. I was in the office trying to figure out who she was with shades and straw hat on. For a minute, I thought it was my wife. 'Bout time I realized who she was, she had already caught Rah seated at the bar with Deanna between his legs kissing him. She cracked him over the head with a gin bottle. He didn't know what hit him until he woke up five days later in a hospital. After she hit him with the bottle, Fat Pat and a few other bouncers had to stop her. The bitch was possessed. She was going to kill him. Deanna vanished like a thief in the night. She'd never set foot in the club again. Zena scared the shit out of her and me. She made it clear, there was nothing more worse or dangerous than a scorned woman, especially a psychopathic one.

I walked into my club from the back entrance. This was the normal entrance for me. It was less hassle. My mere presence of entering the club demanded the attention of every dancer and employee in the room, so I stayed trying to avoid the rush. The back entrance was underneath my office. All I had to do was enter, walk up the flight of stairs, and enter my office.

I called Fat Pat before I arrived to let me in through the back. When I arrived, he was smiling from ear to ear. I knew he had something to tell me. I furrowed my brows like "what happened big man?"

He said excitedly, "Man, yo' boy had to pound on that nigga, Mack Moon." He threw some phantom punches.

"Now why you do that?" I asked sarcastically. I already knew what happened. KC had called me and given me the run down, first thing in the morning, on how Mack Moon had tried to gorilla pimp on one of our girls. Fat Pat knocked him completely out with one punch and threw him out of the club.

Terry Wroten

Pat told me his side of the story. It balanced out with what I'd already known. But you know he exaggerated his role to boost his ego. He added that he'd hit Moon so hard that when he hit the floor, he went into convulsions and was slobbering at the mouth like he was going to die.

"So you pounded the boy like that?" I asked in a disbelievingly manner.

"Man, you know, I stay gettin' it poppin' when a muhfucka get outta line."

We exchanged laughter. I dismissed him back to his duties, but before I got into my office, he said, "Oh yeah! I think I saw Sheila up in here last night, but I'm not for sure. I was too busy icing my hand."

That set a FIVE ALARM FIRE in my head. Oh shit! That bitch probably do know about Candy and on some stakeout type shit. That's why she stayed out all night. My brain started speeding at a hundred miles per hour. I just decided to question KC and see what I could get out of her.

It was dark and quiet inside the office, so that meant KC was at the bar or somewhere around the club. I hit the light and walked over to the monitors on my desk. As soon as I got to the screen, Fat Pat was whispering to KC that I arrived. She smiled. She was working the bar with Ayana and groping her at the same time. She looked into the camera positioned over the bar and finger waved. Her lips read: I'll be up in a few.

I sat in the office going over paperwork and the profits we'd made over the week. All was well and things were looking good. No sooner had I figured how good the club was doing than I had a vision. The office was big enough to use half of it as a studio. I figured I could knock out the back wall and equip soundproof glass around it. I was so into getting the record label up and running, shit was just popping in my head. I sat contemplating my next business move until KC came walking in.

Girl, I Had Enough!

"'Sup, nigga? Why you didn't buzz me in, I know you peeped me comin'." KC's deep voice irritated the hell out of me. She was too gorgeous to be sounding like Mike Tyson. I shook my head. I couldn't knock my sister-in-law's sexual preference, but it was like damn, talk normal.

"You got a key don'tchu?" I asked defensively.

"Sure do."

I stared at her. "Well, you did the right thing by using it. Anyhow, Crazy Lady, if I would have seen or heard you comin', I woulda buzzed you in. Shit, I was in deep thought until you derailed them."

KC walked over and extended her hand. We exchanged hand shakes. "Now, that's more like it. Anyway, we got to talk."

"About what?"

"Me movin'."

"When?"

"In a few months."

"Where to?"

"Hot-lanta."

I chuckled. I didn't know if KC was lying or not. "Who you know down there?"

"Oh, I got some family on my father's side of the family who been tryna get me out there. I figured, I done already fucked as many Cali females as I could. Now, I need a few Georgia Peaches. Nahmean?"

I nodded nonchalantly. KC was a good business partner, but I couldn't knock what she wanted to do with her life. I figured, shit, why not try to give Strokers and Magic City a run for their money?

"I hope it ain't no hard feelings that I'm deciding to up and leave. Even my sister mad at me."

I cracked a one-sided smile. "Oh naw. You know, you'll always be straight with me. Shit, I was thinking, once you get settled, we might could open up a club or two down there. You know in this industry the

183

south is where all the money is at. Anyhow, speaking of your sister, what was she doing here last night?"

KC seethed, "Who told you, Fat Pat's fat ass? Do he ever stop running his mouth around here? But yeah, I had her come get my house keys and take 'em to Donna. Remember Donna? The mix breed bitch I use to fuck with?"

I nodded.

"Okay. She's suppose to be movin' with me, so I had her come get my keys and take 'em to her because you said you weren't comin' in last night. But she was in and out. You know, she don't like being in this place, especially without you."

I smiled. That was all I needed to hear. As long as I knew Shelia wasn't spying or up to no good, I was content. And to add icing to the cake, she was just in and out, so I knew she didn't know about Candy. I decided to change the subject.

"So what you plan on doing when you settle down in the A-T-L? I know fuck a few ho's, but what else?"

CALVIN

33

W hy'd y'all pick this chi-chi frou-frou spot?" I asked the 3IA entering the dining room of Chia's, a posh Thai restaurant in Chinatown section of downtown LA.

The 3IA consisted of three young spies: Hammer, Mouse, and Ali. They were as good as the CIA when it came to spying and getting information. This was why I called them the 3IA (3 Information Agencies). I hired them to spy on Alice and her boyfriend for me. They were specifically put on duty to find out as much information about Alice's boyfriend as possible. I didn't know him from Adam, but knew I had to kill him after pulling a gun on him. I felt it was life or death. Rules of the street: "never pull a gun on a man if you not going to kill him". And after the way he disrespected me in front of my kids, I had to send him to his maker. Not counting the minor fouls he had committed like getting into it with my son in my own house and helping the bitch Alice press charges against me. I was fuming. It was, how could a nigga who just pulled a long stretch get out and work with the police? But the funny thing is, the shit was all a lie!

"How y'all know I ain't want some fried chicken or steak?" I joked, taking my seat.

"We didn't think it really mattered, due to the understanding that we're only here to conduct business," Ali replied with a snide grin spread across his face. He was my kid. He was strictly business. He was the leader of the 3IA. I just knew he was going to be doing all the talking.

"Well, if that's the case, give me what y'all got so I can get on with my business."

"Kick back, Fooliac, you know a nigga just jokin' with yo' crazy ass."

I cracked a one-sided smile. "Oh! I thought maybe now that y'all blew up, y'all probably got too big-headed to spend some quality time with the Negro who put y'all in the game."

"Naw, that ain't even the case, my dude. We up here because we decided to knock out two birds with one storm. See, the Asian Mafia got us on detail watching the owner of this joint to see how much dough he's raking in. They believe he's making more than he's reporting to them. You know, these Asians be with that extortion shit down here in Cali. And from our observation of this spot, the owner ain't paying his protectors their righteous cut. This fool just ain't sellin' sushi and lychee martinis out of here. He's sellin' er' thing. Watch. Look at that fool over there carryin' that tray. Best believe that's more than food."

I shook my head. Unfortunately, I was not convinced. It was not a surprise to me that damn near every real businessman or woman in LA opened up a business front to move everything other than what their business advertised. I decided to change the subject. "Let me hear what you got on Alice's boyfriend."

"All right, look, check game. Alice's boyfriend's name is Tyson. His government name is Tyree Chaplin. He's a Crip from up outta Watts, The Projects. He and Alice grew up together. A bitch named Eve gave me the whole rundown for a bit of nothing. Word is, Tyson supposed to be the nigga who took her virginity, and they been on and off for years. They say she supposedly looked out for the dude while he just served a ten year bid, sending him money, packages, and whatnot."

Girl, I Had Enough!

"Money," I repeated in a stone whisper. I couldn't believe my ears. If Drama Queen was sending him money, it was money I sent or gave to her for the kids. I fumed. My blood pressure shot sky high. I started shaking my head disbelievingly.

"Yeah, money. She supposedly looked out for him while he was locked up, so when he got out, they got back together. A hoodrat named Serena hooked them back up. Now, this the part I don't know if I should tell you or not."

I folded my arms across my chest and snapped my neck from side to side. "Man, just spit it out raw and uncut, I'd rather hear from y'all than anyone else."

Ali let out a deep breath. "Well, word is, she been fuckin' with old boy before he pulled that ten, and your twins might be his."

Two daggers hit my heart repeatedly.

"But they also could be yours, his, or three other niggas. I can only tell you to get a paternity test immediately, my dude."

My heart was racing. Beads of sweat popped through my pores onto my forehead. I wiped the drizzling. I crossed my ankles under the table. Tears rushed to my eyes. I forcefully held them in. My palms began to sweat. And my trigger finger began to inch. It felt like someone was pulling at my heart and I was ready to kill. I didn't care what I had done in the past, or how scorned Alice was from my one mistake. But that bitch was playing with my kids, and that was a NO-NO!

"Well, I still got a worker followin' them around," Ali informed. "If you want, I can call him and find out their whereabouts."

I nodded briskly. Ali called his worker. Alice and Tyson was going to die this night. When Ali closed his cell phone, he looked at me and shook his head. I sensed he was going to say something that was going to stab me in the heart again. I felt it . . .

"Calvin, my boy just informed me that he's at Santa Monica Pier watching Alice and Tyson fucking on the sand under the pier. He say they just got there, so they might be there for a while."

I fumed, tucked in my bottom lip, and shook my head. Santa Monica Pier was the same place Alice and I conceived CJ and Joy. I didn't know what to think. Then, all of sudden, a light popped on in my head. I snapped my fingers and twisted my neck. I looked around the restaurant for all the cameras. I needed an alibi. I spotted all of them. I had to get on camera and show my face. I hopped up from my chair and told Ali to tell his boy to stay put. I strolled over to the hostess table and asked the Asian lady if I could reserve a table for two. I smiled at the cameras the whole time while doing so.

She said, "We have no available tables. One will probably open within the next hour." She had a strong Asian accent.

I bowed. "Can I get the next available one, please!"

She asked, "Name?"

I gave her my ID. "Keep it. I'll be right back. I got to go outside and smoke a cigarette."

I didn't wait on a response. I needed this lady to remember me. As soon as I got out of the restaurant and out of sight, I ran like a felon under hot pursuit to Angel's Lexus. I was glad I chose to borrow her car for the day, because I needed the motor to push me to Santa Monica and back to downtown LA in record breaking time. I needed everything to be done within one hour.

When I made it to the car and started the engine, I flew like a bat out of hell to the freeway. As soon as I got onto the I-10 west, I switched lanes all the way over to the carpool. On the straightaway of the carpool, I pushed the car to 110 mph. I wasn't worried about Highway Patrol or nothing. I grabbed my cell phone with one hand and held the steering wheel with the other. I dialed Angel's cell phone. She answered on the first ring. "Yes. Calvin."

I asked, "Where you at?"

"I'm just making it home. Why?"

Girl, I Had Enough!

"Okay. Look, run to the bathroom, wash up, slide on something nice and meet me at Chai's restaurant in Chinatown. Please, don't ask any questions, just do it. You got a little under a hour."

Angel agreed. I hung up. I then called Rasheed. He answered on the third ring. "What it do, bro?"

"Look, some shit 'bout to go down, so I need you to get my kids from my house and take 'em to your house or Momma's house."

"Calvin, what's the business? What's happening? Let me know something?"

"Rah, it's not the time to be talking over this phone. Just go get my kids!"

"Man, all right! All right! Just be safe whatever you 'bout to do. We gon' be at Momma's house, because Zena and I on bad terms again. The bitch pulled a gun on me."

"Man, just go get my kids."

I hung up. I pushed the Lexus from 110 to 135. I made it to Santa Monica in fifteen minutes tops. I called Ali as I leapt from the car headed toward the pier.

"Speak," he answered.

"Is they still in the same spot?" I asked.

"Hol' on. Mouse, let me see your phone."

Ali dialed his worker up from Mouse's cell phone. I envisioned him holding both phones to his ears. "Yeah, they still there," he informed. I told him to tell his worker that his job was done. Ali did as told. I hung up. From where I stood, on the bike trail, I could see Alice and Tyson. Fucking. He was on top of her pounding away. I chuckled, checked the silencers on both of my .9s, and waited a minute or two for Ali's worker to leave. I didn't need any witnesses. I slid my hoodie over my head and crept slowly upon Alice and Tyson. I did it so good, I made it over two hundred feet unnoticed. Tyson was still on top of her when I appeared out of nowhere like a ghost. He was literally knocking the lining out of

189

her pussy. Alice was in la-la land. Neither of them noticed me.

I came from behind Tyson and kicked him dead in the ass. "Ouch!" he groaned. His whole body locked in pain. He rolled off of Alice onto his back. His asshole was throbbing with pain.

When he looked up at me, I scolded, "See, I've could've shot you in the back, but my old man had always taught me to never hit or shoot a man in the back. That's what a coward will do. A real nigga look his vic in the eyes and tell him where he went wrong. You went wrong by steppin' to me in front of my kids. How could you disrespect me like that over a bitch?"

Pop, pop, pop, pop, pop, pop!

I sent an entourage of bullets into the middle of his forehead. His noodles flew every which way into the sand.

I glanced over at Alice; she was literally shitting on herself. I couldn't do as much talking as I wanted to, so I made it simple.

"When we first started messin' around, it was love at first sight and all was good. You was my boo and my African queen. As time progressed, a nigga made one mistake and you became the devil. You've brought so much pain into my life, but I still loved you and did all I could for you. Shit, I still love you. You are the mother of my kids. But pain is not love. For that you have dealt me a hand I don't wish upon my worst enemy. They say the foundation of life and adversity can make any human being fall from grace, but by faith, one will be able to surpass all the darkness of life's physical and emotional pains. But life with you is a living nightmare, so bitch, burn in hell!"

Pop, pop, pop, pop, pop, pop, pop, pop, pop, pop, pop, pop, pop!
Click.
Click.

I killed Alice and Tyson that night. Emptied a whole clip on both of them. Sad to say, I walked off a proud man. I made it back to Chai's just

Girl, I Had Enough!

in time. Angel had just arrived. I slapped her on the ass. "Hey, Sexy. Who you looking so good for?"

Angel smiled. "You and only you."

I smiled then frowned. This was only a fucking dream . . .

ANGEL

34

I walked into my room with my protruding belly growing by the day. I was four months pregnant, but looked eight. Every pair of jeans I owned, I either couldn't fit or had to wear unzipped. Calvin had been asleep all morning. It was a little past twelve when he'd arisen from a drunken coma. Ever since Alice filed them frivolous charges against him and he was facing life imprisonment, he had started to drink obsessively, literally until he blanked out or threw up. I was seriously worried about him. I loved Calvin. I felt his pain, but I couldn't stand to see him abuse his body and himself. It was like watching a good apple go bad.

One night, Calvin leaned on my shoulder and cried. He said, "Angel, I love you. Love you so much, I set out to impregnate you, set out to marry you in due time, and set out to show you a man can be true to who he is and who he loves. But it seems like every time a Negro try to do the right thang, something go wrong. Drama Queen tryna get a nigga to pull a bid over some shit she know ain't right. I feel if I gotta do life or any time at all, I might as well do it, because I really killed the bitch! Baby, I can't lie. I've been having nightmares every night of how I can just kill this woman. I mean, I know I don't have the guts to do it, but the more I think about it, the more courage I get. Then it's like, what about my kids? What about you? You pregnant. You love me. And you damn sho' been in my corner since day one. Then, it's like I'm a dead-beat dad, constantly bringing kids into this world, knowing that I can't guide them straight. My oldest son is a gang member. Momma stay calling about him. My baby girl, Joy, is stuck between her momma and my bullshit. In a minute, she gon' be looking for love in all the wrong places. Bill, he don't know what to do. That boy just stay to himself. I don't know how he feel about me. If he ain't with his grandfather, he's in his room playing Playstation. He make sure he stay as far away from me as possible. Then, Charles, my son by Charlene, I could only do so much for him because of how I did his mother in the past. And the twins, man, I can shoot myself in the ass. I just don't know where I went wrong or what to think. Should I love 'em? Are they my kids? Can I even trust 'em after all the garbage Alice put in their head? Angel, I'm just going through it, and it feel like a nigga's life is comin' to a end."

After Calvin vented all his frustrations, I found my face flooded with tears. It was a sad story. A story that was too close to home. I was always called a crybaby growing up, but Calvin's situation was more than worth crying for. There was already a far outcry in the black community with fatherless homes, but it seemed like the small amount of black men who tried to be father figures to their children were being denied. Women were rejecting them with disdain, because of past relationships and torment. But when it all came down to it, the child hurt the most. It was a bad situation.

I stood over Calvin with my hands on my hips like a mother does to a child when the child refuses to get up for school. Calvin was wiping sleep from his eyes. I handed him a wet washcloth "'Bout time you get up. It's noon. And breakfast is on the stove."

He nodded drowsily.

"Also, baby, we need to talk, because we gon' have company over in a few hours and I'm really not liking how you stay reminding me to be a strong woman, but you are not being a strong man. I want you to please stop drinking."

194

Girl, I Had Enough!

He removed the covers from his body and stretched upright. He pinched his nose and massaged his forehead like he was having a hangover. He replied, "I know, baby, I know. I'll get it together. It's just hard on me right now."

I flopped on the bed next to him and tapped him on the thigh. "Baby, I know things are hard on you right now, but it's other ways you, well we, can go about things. But you need to get up and go wash up. I told you we're having company in a few hours."

"Who is this company? And why am I finding out at the last minute?"

I gave him the evil eye. "Will you just get your black behind up and move! If I didn't tell you, that means it's a surprise. Now get up!"

Calvin yawned. "Okay." He rubbed his eyes. "But first, let me tell you that I just had another dream about killing Alice. This time I supposedly killed her and her boyfriend on the beach. Youse a doctor, so I need to know is I'm going crazy? Or, at least, tell me what these dreams are tryna tell?"

"I believe the violence is coming from your situation and you bringing yourself to sleep," I informed. "I don't believe you are going crazy. Let's just say you are letting your situation get the best of you."

He cocked his neck from side to side. "Okay. One more question, since you told me to confide in my future wife and baby mama when I'm down."

I sucked the inside of my cheek. "I'm all ears."

"Well, look at every dream I've been having, it's like someway the twins come up. I don't know if it's from my case or what. But I probably need to get a paternity test, so I could know the real. I mean, all my kids got my eyes, except them . . ."

I laughed. "That don't mean they're not yours."

"I know that woman. It's just something pulling at my heart. However, I'ma leave it alone and go hop my black ass in the shower before you kill me."

195

Terry Wroten

I formed my fingers into a gun, pointed them at him, and acted as if I was shooting him. "Yeah, because I'm the only killer in this house."

A snide grin spread across his face. "Yeah, you talking now, but in the bed you sho' don't be calling yourself a killer." He popped me on the ass as he leapt from the bed and headed for the bathroom. "I'm the only one with a gun in this house. So who the real killer?" he asked while holding his crotch and backpedaling into the bathroom.

I smiled. "You, Big Daddy. You, Big Daddy."

He waved me off. "Yeah I know." He slammed the bathroom door. And I went to get ready for our guest.

CALVIN

35

Whoo! That felt so good," I told myself, hopping out of the shower and drying off. I'd already shaved, shitted and trimmed my goatee. I felt so fresh and clean. I'd been living like a vagabond; just laying up sipping on brew and letting life pass me by. I hadn't washed my ass in days. My situation was one I couldn't even wish on my worst enemy, but I knew a change was going to come. Either bad or good, I knew it was going to come.

Just as the thought crossed my mind, I heard a knock come to the door, then I heard a feminine voice. A voice I just knew belonged to my sixteen-year-old daughter. Joy walked into the house and asked Angel, "Where is my daddy?"

Her voice brought sunshine to my life. I smiled from ear to ear as I slid on some jeans. "I'm in the bathroom!" I yelled through the half-cracked door while laying my waves down with my palm and some Murray's.

Joy appeared at the door and turned her head so she couldn't see inside. "Can I come in? Are you dressed?"

I opened the door all the way. I extended my arms. "You better come in and give me a hug. Do you know how much I been through 'cause I can't see my baby girl?"

Terry Wroten

Joy ran in and jumped into my arms. She had her legs wrapped around my waist. She was heavy as hell. She kissed me on the cheek. "Daddy, I miss you."

I nodded. "I know, I really miss you too. But you got to get your big butt down. You not a little girl no more. You can't keep jumping on me like that. Shit, you gon' break my back."

At that very moment, I glanced at Joy and knew it was time for me to pull out the shotgun and keep it in close range. Just within a few months, Joy had blossomed from looking her age to looking twenty-five. She could have passed for a King model. And not only was my daughter voluptuous, she was gorgeous. I told myself, Boy, I'ma really have to get ready to kill me a nigga.

Joy planted her feet back on the floor and broke our embrace. She backpedaled and closed the bathroom door. She looked me in the eyes and said, "Daddy, I'm sorry." Tears rushed to her eyes. "I didn't want to do it. Momma made me."

I sat on the toilet and knelt in front of her. I held her real tight to let her know I loved her regardless of what she did wrong, but that was the problem, she didn't do anything wrong. She told the truth after her mother tried to force her to lie. I whispered in her ear. "I know, Baby Girl. You didn't do anything wrong. Don't cry." I wiped her tears with my thumb and kissed her on the forehead. I didn't realize my daughter was going through it as much as me. It was a wake-up call for me. I had to pull myself together. Drinking wasn't going to solve anything. I felt awful for even allowing myself to fall so low. I was one sip away from becoming a wino/bottlehead.

"Daddy, I don't want you to go to jail," my daughter sobbed. "I swear, I hate my mama for this. But don't tell CJ I told you this, but he said if you do to jail, he gon' kill Momma's boyfriend. I feel the same way. You the best father anyone could ever ask for."

I was at a loss for words. Once again, our kids were caught up in the middle of our bullshit. It was like, "God please have mercy on me. Shit,,

198

Girl, I Had Enough!

if not on me, on my kids!"

"Don't worry baby, Daddy ain't doing no time. Byrd ain't going to let me. If I do any time, it will be because you're not supposed to be here. And if I got to do some time to see my daughter, so be it."

Joy smiled and tightened her grip around me. "Well, the restraining order says you can't come so many feet near me. It don't say I got to stay so many feet away from you."

I laughed. "Ha! Good one. Anyway, how you get here?"

"Well, Lola somehow got in touch with Charlene. Charlene called Poppa. Poppa called me and told me to pack my stuff for the weekend. Somehow he talked Momma into letting us stay the weekend. Seems like granddaddy is the only person she likes on your side of the family."

"Yeah, that's because he never takes sides and give her anything she wants."

"So Poppa came and got me and Bill this morning. The twins didn't want to come. They wanted to stay with Momma and her boyfriend, who I swear I can't stand. I think they didn't want to come because I be telling them, if you go to jail it's all because of them . . ."

"Don't tell them that. That ain't nice. It wouldn't be their fault."

"Dad, yes it will. I told them don't lie for Momma, to tell the truth. But they didn't listen. Now, I'm the enemy of the state in that house. You know, Bill is a loner, so me and him been getting along good, because I feel like a loner too."

I held her tighter. "Baby, you ain't a loner, you got me, and I'm on your team always. Like I always tell you, I'll never leave you, and I promise. We just got to get over this, and things will get better."

She nodded. "So when we made it to granddaddy's house we put our stuff up, then Charlene came and got us. Daddy, watch when you see Charles, that boy is taller than CJ and slim just like you. He ain't all big like CJ. CJ should be a football player or something."

I thought I heard some more people in the living room, but I figured it to be our neighbor Connie. She came over everyday to check on

Angel and me. But as soon as I figured it wasn't her, a knock came to the bathroom door. I was kneeling in front of Joy. It was Charlene, Charles, CJ, and Angel all standing at the entrance. I felt tears rush to my eyes. My youngest son was me all over again. I hadn't seen him in about a year. I stood up and hugged him. Like Joy had stated, he was taller than CJ. The boy stood about six-foot-seven and was only fourteen.

I looked over at CJ and hugged him. I was semi-upset with him, but he was still my son. He wasn't draped in blue, as I'd come to learn he was known to be, but his blue LA Dodger's fitted hat worn turned to the back and tilted to the left signaled he was a Crip. I knew I had to talk to him sooner rather than later. There were some kids you could look at and see they were at a crossroads; there were others you just knew they'd decided to be gangsters. CJ was at a crossroads, and I knew it was my duty as his father to steer him straight. He was only acting out because he saw his mother and I act out most of his life.

Charlene chimed in. "I want a hug too."

I glanced at Angel and she signaled with her head to gon' ahead. A real boss lady, she had her arms folded across her chest smiling. She was showing no disdain or animosity toward Charlene. It was all good. Charlie Baltimore and Ja Rule said it best: "Every thug needs a lady." And every thug needs a down-ass bitch.

I extended my arms to Charlene and she fell into them. We hugged for a good minute, neither one of us wanting to let go. It was like, damn, so many tears, and so many problems, but here we still standing tall with a young man to raise. My chest rested against hers as we hugged. Charlene was a small woman, five feet tall, but she was a giant at heart. She was a gorgeous woman who packed more bodily impact than an NFL highlight reel. And even though she was forty, she looked no more than twenty. Her mocha face still had a youthful glow to it. It felt good having such a beautiful and caring baby momma.

We hugged until tears flooded her face. I looked at Angel and she was smiling. Somehow, she'd put this all together. She grabbed all the

Girl, I Had Enough!

kids and told them, "Y'all come on. Let's go get ready to go shopping while Charlene and y'all father talk."

At that very moment, I realized my middle son was missing. I looked at CJ and asked, "Where's Bill?"

He pointed toward the living room. "Up in there, sitting on the floor, playing your Playstation 3."

I told Charlene to stay put and marched directly into the living room. Bill was a game fanatic. He was one of them kids who didn't care where he was at, if there was a game in sight, he was going to hop on it. Also, out of all my kids, Bill was the only one who had to wear glasses. And for his age, fifteen, he was quite short at five-foot-two. Compared to my two other sons, he was a midget, but I knew he was taking after his uncle. Rasheed was the same height at about that age fifteen, sixteen. He was a late bloomer, and Bill was too.

"So you couldn't come say 'what's up Dad' before you hopped on my game, huh?" I said hopping in front of the plasma television.

"Aw, Dad, you blocking the TV. You going to make me lose." He looked up at me, trying to look through me to see the television screen.

I frowned. "So this game is more important than me?"

Bill paused the game and leapt up. He gave me a hug. "I miss you, Dad." He still had his eyes glued to the television.

I smiled. "Seems to me that you are just saying that to get back to your game. But since we gon' be together all day, I'ma let you have fun while I go talk to Charlene."

Bill flopped back down on the floor, folded his legs Indian style, and turned back to the game like I'd never bothered him. I heard CJ snicker, "Nerd." He thought he was mumbling to himself, but he had his Discman playing. He was louder than he'd thought. I popped him in back of the head. He turned the volume down. "What was all that for?" he asked.

"Don't be calling your brother a nerd," I said over my shoulders.

"Yeah, that's not nice, CJ," Angel added.

Terry Wroten

I ended up back in the room with Charlene. She still had tears in her eyes. I'd put Charlene though a lot. Off top, I lied to her, told her I was single with no kids, when in fact, I was married with two kids and one on the way. I met Charlene through one of Rasheed's many ex-girlfriends, Rhonda. Rhonda was a middle school teacher, and so was Charlene. They worked at the same school. Knowing Charlene's occupation, I lied about everything: my marital status, my kids, my occupation, and my name. To her, my name was Charles, which was Poppa's father's name. She would eventually give the name to our son. I was sports agent, who was single with no kids and a degree in communications. However, at the time, I was a drug lord, transporting cocaine from state to state, city to city. I was married with two beautiful children. And I'd never spent a day in college.

"Calvin, what you did to me was wrong as two left shoes. You played me like a slot machine in Vegas. I've been hurt for years, because I have never and will never fall for a man the way I did for you. I've hated you for so long, it's killing me softly, because every time I see Charles I see you."

I walked over to Charlene after I slid on the rest of my clothes and held her in my arms. "Charlene, like I've always told you, I never intended to hurt you. I was young and wasn't using my head. And even though you probably hate me forever and a day, I understand. But I want you to know, I'll always respect and love you. You held strong even after I tried my damndest to get you to have an abortion, and I'm glad you did. I love you and my son. Shit, it look like in a few years, his ass gon' be playing in the NBA."

"Yeah, I hope so," Charlene declared. "He's already one of the best in the state. I'm so proud of him. You should of heard him tryna get on CJ – 'Man, you need to play some football or something.' CJ dismissed him. 'Homey, I'ma rappa turned singa'."

Girl, I Had Enough!

I nodded. Trey had given me a demo of some songs Trevon and CJ had recorded for his start-up record label. I was so devastated from my situation, I popped it in the disc player, but never pressed play.

"Anyhow, back to what I was saying. Calvin, you did me bad; so bad, that I didn't know if I wanted to Lorena Bobbitt you or swallow a bottle of pills. I was so fed up, I plotted evil against you. I was scheming, but luckily I never had the guts to follow through. And the one time I did follow through it backfired, because calling that girl is something I really wish I didn't do. I didn't know she was crazy. It seems like I opened up a can of worms, and it's not only you being affected. It's all of us. I didn't know the woman was trying to get you sent to prison. I must say, when a woman's fed up, she'll do the harshest things, but you are one hell of a father. I gots to give you that much. So I'm here let you know Charles and I are in your corner. And I thought I'd tell you, you got a good woman. Please, treat her right, because as you already know, a good girl can turn bad real fast. Look at me, I'm damaged goods."

I kissed Charlene on the forehead. "Baby, you ain't damaged goods. Youse actually a woman most man dream of having. And if I woulda known back then what I know now, youse a keeper. A prize trophy. So remember, what don't kill us, only makes us stronger. You are nowhere near damaged goods, unless you're on the same level as Alice, which you are not. You just feel like that, because now you know how to see through the bullshit us men play. And just so happens you just ain't found the right one, so you starting to feel as if it's you when it's simply not. Woman, youse one of a kind. Don't ever let me hear you say youse damaged goods. You understand?"

Charlene nodded. I kissed her on the forehead again. "Well, let's go do what you women like doing the most. Shit, if my boys weren't here, I'd let the three women in my life go shopping for us. By the way, I'm glad you and Lola are seeing eye to eye. I need that right about now. Thank you."

Terry Wroten

Charlene mushed her index finger in the middle of my forehead. "Real boss ladies work together, because at the end of the day, we know what we want and what we got to do to get it. "She cracked a one-sided smile and walked off. It wasn't all good, but it wasn't all bad. I felt a little at ease.

CALVIN

36

I spent the whole day in the Fox Hills Mall with Angel, Charlene and my kids. It was a quarter-to-nine and closing time when we left. I gave the kids $1000 each. I even gave Joy an extra $2000 to get the twins what they liked. Charlene and Angel didn't want anything. They were content with themselves. They were just glad to see me and the kids have a good time. It was a trip when I found out that Charles wore a size seventeen shoe. I couldn't believe it. My son was on his way to passing up Shaq.

We left the mall and went to Hometown Buffet. We were having a good time. I hadn't felt so good in a long time, but this good feeling only lasted so long.

Joy left the table to go fill her plate for the fourth time. The girl was out-eating everyone at the table, even CJ. I watched her as she filled her plate, thinking how she was eating like Alice wasn't feeding her at home. Then, the thought of pregnancy crossed my mind. Pregnancy was like a plague in my family; if one person got pregnant, it was widespread. Next thing you know, this person was pregnant, that person was pregnant, and everyone was giving birth about the same time.

I watched Joy put fried chicken, barbeque ribs, mashed potatoes, macaroni and cheese, and corn bread on her plate. Then, out of nowhere, a brother about my age emerged and wrapped his arms around her shoulders. He whispered something in her ear.

She looked up at him and smiled. I instantly thought, *this fool tryna mack my daughter*. I leapt up so fast, everyone at the table looked at me as if I'd lost my mind. I did not say one word. My mind had snapped. I'd already told myself I was going to have to kill a nigga over my daughter. I nudged my waist with my elbow to make sure my gun was holstered there. I was glad I told myself *don't leave home without it*. I felt I didn't need it, since I was going to be spending the day with my children, but knowing CJ had been hanging with the Crips, I wasn't going to let anyone step to my son. For lack of definition, I didn't feel complete without it.

I made it over to the buffet where Joy was standing and grabbed the dude's arm from around my daughter. "Ay bruh, ain't you too old to be tryna mack on my sixteen-year-old daughter?" I said, stepping between him and Joy.

He backpedaled and threw his hands in the air like I was the police. For a minute, I thought he was going to try to swing, but he said, "Naw, it ain't even like that. My wife and kids are sitting right over there." He pointed to his wife and kids. "I watched Joy grow up."

"Oh! Byron, what's up?" CJ said interrupting. They exchanged handshakes and a brisk manly hug. I was confused. Who was this guy?

CJ turned to me. "Dad, this is Byron. Momma's ex-boyfriend. The cool one."

I nodded.

"And Byron, this my dad, Big Calvin."

Byron extended his hand. We exchanged handshakes. He looked me dead in my eyes. "Calvin, I have daughters myself, so I know where you coming from. It was no disrespect intended. And I hope none was taken."

I made eye contact back with him. "Oh, best believe, after hearing my son talk highly of you, none was taken. Just doing what I believe my father would do."

Girl, I Had Enough!

Byron nodded. "I understand."

'Bout this time, Angel, Charlene and my other two sons had made it over. "Bill, what's up my man," Byron said, holding his hand out so Bill could slap him five.

Bill slapped him five and said, "Man, what happened to the game?"

Byron screwed his face. "Man, your mama didn't give you that game?"

"Yep. She gave me one, but said it was from her new boyfriend."

"Was it Grand Theft Auto?"

"Yep."

"Okay. That came from me, but I'ma send you another one through your dad or somebody else. Is that cool with you?"

Bill smiled. "Yep." He gave Byron a high five and walked off.

Byron's wife walked up. She looked Ethiopian and was fine as wine. I rubbed my eyes, trying my best not to stare. She asked Byron, "Honey, everything okay?" in a strong Ethiopian accent.

Byron kissed her gently on the lips. "Yes. Baby, everything is fine. Just go back to the table. No questions asked." He looked at me. "Now, Calvin, it's only by the grace of God that I've run into you. I need to talk to you man to man, but not in front of your family. Can we talk in the men's room?"

I didn't know Byron from Adam, but he sounded sincere. I looked at my family and told them go back and eat. I followed Byron to the men's room, but when he got inside, he changed his mind on whatever he was going to tell me.

"Look, bruh, I got some heartfelt shit I need to share with you, but being the humble man that I am, I will never play with a man's family, so since I know you are out having a good time with your family, I must do it this way. First, do you have a fax number? Because I have some stuff I need you to check out. I don't live here in Cali no more, but what I'm down here for, you could help. I can't go into details right now, but give me your fax number and I'll have everything faxed to you before

207

you make it home. My wife's mom stay around the corner, so I'ma fax the stuff straight to you."

I furrowed my brows. I didn't know what the hell Byron was talking about, but I was curious as hell to find out. I just knew it had something to do with Alice. She was the only thing we had in common. With the quickness, I slid him Angel's fax number.

He patted me on the back. "I know this is an awkward moment, but you'll see where I'm coming from as soon as you get home."

We shook hands and went our separate ways. He called over his shoulders "Tell Bill I will send that game through you as soon as possible."

I gave him the thumbs up and went to finish dining with my family. All eyes were on me when I returned back to the table. Everyone wanted to know what was up. Shit, I didn't know myself. My mind was racing. I was thinking of everything possible. It could have been anything, but I tried to downplay everything until we made it home.

When we arrived home, I ran straight to Angel's study lounge and found the green light flashing on her fax machine. I picked up the papers Byron had faxed and sat at Angel's desk reading over everything. The opening letter read:

Dear Calvin,

Brother, the next few pages you are about to read are very devastating and mind-blowing. They will damage most brothers mentally, physically, and emotionally. This was the reason why I couldn't explain it to you earlier, but the following pages goes as follow . . .

A letter from the child support folks saying I owe them $6500 and a letter I wrote Alice awhile back, but she never wrote or got back to me.

Bruh, after you read these papers give me a call so we could work something out . . .

Thanks!

Byron Woods

Girl, I Had Enough!

I flipped the page. Off top, I spotted a California certified seal stamped on the paper. Below it, read:

This notice serves as a request that you pay Mrs. Alice Williams $6,500 in back child support. It is to our knowledge that you are the biological father of Alexia Williams, age nine, and Alexis Williams, age nine.

I found myself glancing at the letter and at the barrel of my gun. My initial thought was to pull the trigger. I thought about committing suicide. My heart was racing. I was contemplating evil. Okay, if I just go kill that bitch right now, take all the money and put it in Angel's account so she could take care all the kids, I'll be all right. Then, when the police come, fuck it! Go out with a bang, like a G. I started thinking the craziest shit. It felt like my heart was being ripped out of my chest in slow motion. I told myself I need a drink, but I didn't budge. I moved on to Byron's letter. It was dated two-and-a-half years back.

Dear Alice,

Today, I get home and find a letter from the child support people. The letter read: Dear Mr. Byron Woods, the notice services as a request that you pay Mrs. Alice Williams $6,500 in back child support. It is to our knowledge that you are biological father of Alexia Williams, age nine, and Alexus Williams, age nine . . .

The letter went on to say that if I don't pay you all this goddamn money, they gon' lock my black ass up. You play these childish-ass games and call the folks on me. You told me straight out the girls are your husband's, but I knew something was up when you kept trying to say it's a 50/50 chance. But then, you think I don't know you was also fucking my best friend behind my back. Larry told me everything. You are trifling, scandalous, and mischievous for this. A straight-up larcenous-ass bitch!

Man, Alice, I never thought it'll ever come down to some bullshit like this. If Alexia and Alexis are my daughters, you should of been woman enough to tell me. You were woman enough to open your legs and mouth to me, and no telling who else! Man, you are one scandalous bitch! I feel like bussin' yo' muhfuckin head with a Corona bottle, then cutting your face with the glass. This is why I've decided to write you this letter as opposed to confronting you. I just pray to God that you call them folks and let them know the real, that I ain't the father!

I'd always told myself no matter what I do in life, I would take cares of mines. You denied me that right. You didn't want me to ruin your stability. I respected your call. It's killing me knowing that after all these years, you pull this triflin'-ass shit. I mean, damn, do you even care that a nigga have a family now? God knows I respect you and yours, but what if I call your husband and send him these papers?

I tried to move on with my life, but how do you tell a child the man who been interacting with them as their father, isn't? How do you even tell the man? Bad enough when I saw you at the mall two months ago, I looked at them girls and knew they were mine. Something in my heart told me, but I couldn't do nothing. I felt less than a man. I'm not a deadbeat father! I take care all of my kids. This is why it is hard for me to accept what you are pulling. I mean, I'd rather go back to hustling before I let a kid of mines go without.

To add fuel to the fire, you gave these folks the satisfaction of adding my name, another nigger to the "HE AIN'T SHIT" list, when in fact, you know I love the kids; even your kids. My life for theirs any day. Then, these muhfuckas talking about locking a nigga up like it's my fault that you got on welfare. I know for a fact your husband is a stand-up man from the way your kids, especially CJ and Joy, talk about him. So I know you just tryna work a nigga. Youse a greedy-ass bitch!

However, I'ma leave this in the hands of the Lord, but I do ask that you find it somewhere in your heart to call these people and tell 'em you made a mistake. Alice, I don't need this kind of drama. I moved all the way out here to D.C., so I could have a better life. Please, don't try

Girl, I Had Enough!

to make it miserable, because I'd rather burn in hell before I let you . . .

Have a nice life,

Byron

My whole body began to shake like I was having a nervous break-down. I started throwing phantom punches. The love I held for my daughters were as strong as any parent's. I had my doubts and was hurt-ing within, but nothing beats the pain of knowing the possibilities of them not being mine was greater than I thought or could imagine. I could have killed Alice. I wanted to kill Alice! I was at the point of no return. I hated her! Even the thought of her name made me rave. I threw phantom punches until my mind went blank.

I went into a dark rage. I punched holes into the wall and screamed, "Why!" Tears flooded my face. My heart was crushed. I wished I had never received them damn papers.

"Bitch, how could you do this me?"

"You lied!"

"I knew it . . ."

When I snapped back to reality, my hands were filled with blood; Charlene, Angel, and my kids were all staring at me in utter shock. The pain I felt was unexplainable My heartbeat had quickened. It felt like I was having a heart attack and hyperventilating at the same time. It felt like a piece of me was missing. I treasured the growth of the twins, even though they probably weren't mine. I dropped to my knees and sobbed, "Why?!? Why me?"

Angel cautiously walked over and placed my head on her thigh. She didn't know the cause of my sudden out burst, but she knew whatever it was had broken me down as a man. She asked, "What's wrong?" in a concerned voice.

Silence. I couldn't answer. I just handed her the letter. "Read it," I sobbed between breaths of air. I tried to take a minute to breathe and pull myself together for my kids, but I felt like the walls were closing in on me. Like my lungs were my pride and joy. The female version of Rasheed and I. I was a man whose ego had been crushed. The pain was tenfold any other pain I'd experienced in life. It was fire in my veins. How in the hell was I supposed to tell two innocent little girls that the man they know as father might not be their father?

I sat for hours to myself. After Angel read the letter, Charlene picked it up. After her it went down the line to my kids. They were old enough to grasp the situation. I stood on my knees and sobbed all the way to the wee hours.

When I looked up, Charlene and the kids were gone. They'd all said their farewells hours back, but I was so gone, I just dismissed them. Charlene didn't want the kids to see me as such; neither did Angel. I couldn't blame them. I was a hot mess. I had to pull myself together. The twins are my daughters, I thought. Fuck what some nigga or some bitch say, they are mines!

My mind was speeding. It felt like I was going crazy. I needed some liquor. I needed to escape reality. Drama Queen was getting the best of me.

It was quarter to three when I flopped on the couch in the living room with one foot on the floor and the other stretched outward. Angel was in the kitchen putting the finishing touches on some fried chicken. I was pressed. I couldn't make it to the shooting range, so my next best option was a fifth of Easy Jesus and a six-pack of Heineken. I wished I had a Swisher Sweet blunt and some potent marijuana. I did not want to deal with the hand I'd been dealt. I felt a good run was better than a bad stand.

When Angel finished cooking, she served dinner. I didn't really get to eat at Hometown Buffet, so I was hungry as three bears. I was laid up on the couch La-Z-boy style. One fourth of the Easy Jesus and Heinekens were gone. I was a little buzzed and feeling good. Easy Jesus was known to ease my problems. Made me forget why I was pressed in the

Girl, I Had Enough!

first place. It wasn't long before I realized why so many blacks folks in the ghetto got drunk. It was like, you forget all your troubles. You forget everything until the booze wears off.

I threw Angel's fried chicken back like it was my last meal on the streets and I was headed to prison. I knew it was bad to eat while drinking, but I didn't care. I ate and drank. By the time I looked up, the fifth was half empty and I was on my fourth Heineken.

Angel looked at me and shook her head. "You'd better slow down. Calvin, you drinking that stuff like it's water."

I guffawed. I was drunk as a skunk. "Aww, baby, this shit ain't nothing. I can drink this with ease." I was talking out of the side of my neck.

Angel folded her arms under her breasts and shook her head. "Okay, Mr. Billy Bad Ass, I don't want to hear your mouth in the morning."

I sucked my teeth. "Now have you ever seen me wake up with any problems?" I asked sarcastically.

Angel grabbed the plate filled with chicken bones and headed back to the kitchen. "That's the problem, Calvin," she called over her shoulder. "You are not a drunk. You are drinking because you are letting Alice and your problems take you under. You are sinking like the Titanic and don't seems to care. Calvin, you can't run from reality, baby."

I agreed. "Yeah, I know, Lola." I was in and out now. I started saying anything that came to mind. "Baby, I ain't got nothing to run from. With you in my life, it's all peaches and cream."

I start mimicking Nelly's and Kelly Rowland's remix of Patti LaBelle's song "Love You": "Angel, I love you. Angel, I need you. Angel, I, I love you, I do ... " I murdered the song, but you couldn't tell me I wasn't the shit.

I was so gone, I started throwing my hands in the air like a gang member. In a mock-gangster tone I started shouting, "WESTSIDE!" I threw up the "W".

"I don't give a fuck! WESTSIDE!"

Terry Wroten

Angel came storming back into the living room with her arms folded across her chest. She had a disgusted look on her face. "Calvin, this is not no goddamn house party. And damn sho' not the ghetto! I have working-class neighbors. And this is a working-class community!"

Angel was too uptight for my drunken taste. I leapt up from the couch, bounced my shoulders up and down, and walked over to her. When I made it within nose length of her, I threw my hands up in the air like "hey!". I stood in my B-boy stance like, "how you like me now?"

Angel shoved passed me and grabbed the rest of the Easy Jesus and two Heinekens. "You can not drink no more in this house! If I got to wear the dick in this relationship to get you to act right, so be it!"

"Party pooper," I shot as she grabbed the booze and headed back into the kitchen.

I was still dancing with my hands in the air throwing up the "W" and leaning like a cholo. I did this for a minute, then realized there was no music on. I walked over to the entertainment system and hit the on switch. My son's and Trey Love's single came blasting through the speakers. I had forgotten Trey had given me a demo. I turned the volume up. Fuck the neighbors! Bitch! *This my muhfuckin' son*, I thought.

I really started wildin' out. "Yeeeeeeeeeeeeeaaaaaaaaaaahhhhhhhh!"

"That's my muhfuckin son!"

"WESTSIDE!"

"WESTSIDE!"

Angel was now furious. I'd done the most! She snaked by me and turned the system off. I was in the middle of the floor doing the Crip Walk, the 2 step, the Motorcycle, and the Electric Slide.

She fumed. "I will not sit here and let you humiliate me," she barked. "You're acting like you are seventeen and insolent! Now I see why you didn't drink at first. The shit turn you into a beast. You are like night and day when you're intoxicated! Calvin, you need to call it a night."

Angel was right. The liquor had caught up with me. I was out of control and being totally disrespectful to her and her domain. I kissed her

214

Girl, I Had Enough!

on the forehead, apologized for being so mean and inconsiderate, and staggered to the bedroom. As soon as I flopped on the bed, I was out.

In the morning, I found myself kneeling over the toilet throwing up all the particles of fried chicken I had consumed, while Angel stood over me with her arms folded across her chest talking shit. The combination of her yapping, the horrible smell reeking from the toilet, the pain throbbing in my head, and the taste of my breath would eventually sum up my drinking career. I couldn't run from reality no more, because the fact was, it was still going to be there when the buzz wore off.

Every time I tried to shake off the throbbing pain in my head it got worse. It felt like someone had clubbed me over the head with a brick. And with Angel not showing any remorse or mercy with her mouth, I was doomed.

"I tried to warn you, Mr. Billy Bad Ass. But nooooo! You wanted to be Mr. Tough Guy. So you need to be punished for the way you carried yourself last night. I hope the drinking god come down on you twice as hard. Might make you not want to drink no more. I just hope you learn your lesson. I'm a doctor. I should know how to help you. Well, even if I do, I think, you need to suffer a little longer."

Angel was getting on my last nerve. I was too weak to keep slamming the bathroom door in her face. I just had to accept my punishment and roll with the punches.

"Calvin, you need to understand, you can't run from life. You got to take each punch and get stronger. I know, you are feeling a little down, but this is just karma. You are being punished for all the bad you did coming up. If you could give it, you could get it. You did a lot of women dirty, and one is just going to the extreme to pay you back. You got to look at it as karma and stay strong, because the more you fall, the more she win. Now, even if you're not Alexia and Alexis's biological father —and we can easily get a test if that will stop your 'what if' theories and doubts—regardless of the outcome, the twins are still yours."

Terry Wroten

I nodded to everything Angel was saying while my face was still glued to the bowl. After she finished lecturing, she brought me something to coat my stomach. "Here, take this. It should help."

I didn't know what she was handing me and didn't care. I just knew one thing and one thing only: I was staying my black ass as far away from Easy Jesus and any other form of liquor. I decided I had deal with all the punches life threw at me sober and as a man. It was time to step up to the plate and handle business.

ALICE

37

"ome on, Alice!" Tyson yelled, tugging my shoulders. "Man, get yo' ass up! The baby been crying all morning, and all yo' ass do is sleep. Cuzz, getta fuck up! Plus, you must've forgot that you got court today."

I was exhausted. I'd just given birth to my one-and-a-half month old daughter, Tyra Chaplin. I'd been up all month breastfeeding, changing diapers, and the whole nine while Tyson did nothing but sit on his ass and complain all the damn time. I'd told myself the dick was good, but a nigga just laying up living off of me and my hustles weren't cool. Bad enough my four main sponsors were trying their best to cut me off. The government was saying since I was married to Calvin, I didn't need to be on welfare. Calvin filed a complaint to SSI, telling them I was using them and our son just to defraud the system. He even wrote a letter to our divorce judge—well, it wasn't him personally, but he signed it. Shalon, his attorney and Byrd's wife, wrote it. The bitch had the nerves to say I was a larcenous, mischievous, fraudulent swindler, who has abused the government and SSI by submitting false documents stating Bill Williams is mentally ill, when in fact he's an honor roll student. So that was two of my sponsors that I was surely having problems with. And my social worker wasn't making things any better. She was working with Shalon and Calvin, talking about I'm abusing tax payer's

Terry Wroten

My third sponsor was Byron. Truthfully speaking, I was just using him because I could. He was a patsy. He knew he wasn't the father of the twins. I'd already conceived when I started fucking him, but if he was too dumb to do the math... Like they say, "you play with pussy, you get fucked". He was a married man when we met. He pulled the same shit on me that Calvin pulled on Charlene, but he thought I wasn't going to find out. Well, I threw him for a loop just like I did to Calvin. Plus, I was pregnant. I told him straight out, "What's good for the thug is better for the thugette." I let him think he was getting off easy until I sicced the child support on his ass. After two straight years of playing faithfully, I guess, his pockets started to get low, because all of a sudden he filed for a paternity test with the courts and didn't care if his wife found out.

And my last and final sponsor, MY MAIN SPONSOR! The man I love to hate had pulled all the way out. He wasn't doing nothing. He stopped paying the bills, child support, my car note, and luckily, the house was already paid for. He even filed for custody of our kids and a paternity test for the twins. I told him to kiss my ass, and beat it with the bullshit. Even if the twins weren't his, he signed the birth certificates.

He frowned. "Yeah bitch, whatever," and walked off.

"That's Mrs. Bitch to you," I scolded as he walked off. "And pull ya drawls outta ya ass, 'cause you'll always be paying for this pussy. So slap ya self with ya dick, nigga, cause you gettin' fucked in the ass with mines."

He flipped me the bird and kept walking . . .

I leapt from bed and headed straight to the bathroom. I had to pee real bad! I sat on the toilet and released the build up with the door wide open. I was watching Tyson for the first time walk around carrying Tyra in his arms. I wondered how long he had been up. Tyra's days and nights were all mixed up. I looked like Spot from the heavy bags I had under my eyes. I couldn't tell you the last time I got a good night's sleep.

Girl, I Had Enough!

"'Bout time yo' black ass do something useful around here," I told Tyson as I flushed the toilet and started running water to take a quick shower. "'Cause yo' dick might be good, but dick come a dime a dozen. You gots to start doin' something. Get a job, a hustle, or something!"

Tyson looked over his shoulders, then around the room as if saying "who are you talking to"? I slid out of my night clothes and said, "I'm talking to you."

He looked down at the baby, then back at me. "Who, me?" he thumbed to himself.

"Tyson, who else can I be talking to?"

"To yo' goddamn self," Tyson taunted, "because if I recall right, we both living off the next nigga and we both ain't doing shit! So what you need to do is hop yo' ass in that shower and get to that court while the kids downstairs waiting on you, and while I feel like watching the baby."

I didn't feel like arguing with Tyson, so I decided to let the topic go. I was growing tired and fed up with his shit. Like my momma use to tell my daddy, "Nigga, I could do bad on my own". It's only a matter of time before enough is enough.

At times, I felt bad for doing the things I did to Calvin. Despite his one mistake, I couldn't lie, he was a damn good man and father to the kids. I was always told a "a good man is hard to find", and I found this to be true. Calvin was truly a good man, but I was up shit's creek with him, so the more I thought about not being able to have him back, the more fed up I became with him. And to add fuel to the fire, that doctor bitch of his was pregnant; seven months! I felt like socking that fat bitch in the stomach at the last court date, but she was lucky the bailiff escorted us all out. However, that was at the criminal court building. Today was for our divorce, and I was hoping the judge granted me alimony, the house, the cars, the kids, the dogs. I felt like Kelly Price; I wanted it all. And by hook or crook, I was going to get what I wanted. I was a go-getter.

Terry Wroten

"Alice, man, hurry up and get yo' ass out the shower!" Tyson's yelling knocked me out of thought. "Yo' ass got exactly thirty minutes to make it to that court. Whatta fuck taking so long?"

I was about to explode. Tyson just didn't know how much he was walking on thin ice. I have never been a woman to support a man. Men were the breadwinners, so it was their duty to support me. I don't know what Tyson was thinking, but he had me twisted like a contortionist.

I turned off the water, reached outside the shower, and grabbed a dry-off towel. As I dried off, I glanced at Tyson sitting at the edge of the bed gawking me. "You sho' is rushin' me to get out my own house. You act like you 'bout to have company or something. I'll get to the court when I get there."

"Bitch, I was just tryna help yo' stupid ass. But I know one thing, I'm not yo' punk-ass husband. You ain't gon talk to me no kinda way. I'll knock yo' ass out!"

I taunted, "You don't scare me."

"Bitch, just go handle your business before I hurt you."

I dismissed his threat. "I'm not gon' be too many of your bitches."

"Man, I don't want to hear that shit!" he spat. "If I wanted to fuck a bitch outside or inside this house, I'll fuck her in front of you. I'm just hoping you'll hurry up and getta fuck on and come back, so I could getta fuck outta this house."

I dismissed him. "Yeah whatever."

I got dressed and met the kids downstairs. Bill had his eyes glued to his Game Cube. The twins were playing hot-hands. And Joy was sitting elbows to knees and palms to cheek like she was bored. She rolled her eyes as I entered the living room.

"Bitch, I don't know what you rollin' yo' eyes for. You got something to say? 'Cause right about now, I'll fuck you up, ho!"

"Psst! You ain't gon' touch me."

As soon as I was 'bout to haul off and slap the heifer, Tyson grabbed my arm. "Alice, wait 'til you come back from court before you put yo'

Girl, I Had Enough!

hands on the girl. You need to go see what them people are talking about so we'll know what we gotta do."

Tyson was right. I straightened myself up, rolled my eyes back at Joy, and told her she best watch her mouth. The little bitch thought she was grown. I told the kids, "Let's go!"

CHARLENE

38

Charles and I patiently waited down the street from Alice's house. We were in my car waiting for her to pull off. It had been three long months since I'd found out how trifling she really was. I wasn't one to pass judgment, but this woman was wrong! I knew Calvin wasn't a saint, but he didn't deserve all the drama and nonsense Alice was putting him through. At first, I thought he was getting everything he deserved, but Alice was going overboard. My conscience wouldn't let me sleep at night. Most days I called in to work sick, because it was like I hadn't had any sleep in months. I couldn't get over the fact that she was using her children as pawns to get to him. I couldn't get over the fact that she pressed charges on him for a crime he did not commit. He was being charged with attempted murder, but no one was injured. I had three brothers in prison doing life sentences for crimes they didn't commit where women lied to the police. I also couldn't get over the fact that the twins were MAYBES after I'd taken them in as my son's sisters and my daughters. I was fed up with Alice's shit. Had been for years, but never to the point where I was scheming to do any evil. However, when a woman's fed up, she'll do just about anything to get revenge or destroy her problem or problems.

I was working at a continuation school for troubled teens as a substitute teacher for a semester. One of my students named Monica always stayed in class during nutrition and lunch. I left my doors open for my students, so they wouldn't have to be out in the hot sun if they didn't want to. Most kids didn't care how cold or hot it was, they were just glad to be out of class and away from school work, but not Monica. She came faithfully and sat in the nook of the classroom, reading various books. To me, this was surprising, because kids weren't into reading like my generation was when we were coming up. The new generation felt if it wasn't a text message or e-mail, they weren't reading it, let alone a book. However, Monica was different from her peers. I watched her everyday for about a week straight read books by authors I'd never heard of, like: Hoodrat by K'wan, Entangled by K-Elliot, Dutch by Terri Woods, Let That Be The Reason by Vickie Stringer, and one by an author named Kisha Green.

Now, I was a well-read person. I'd never heard of any of these authors, and I was curious to know who they were and what they wrote? I approached Monica one afternoon and asked her what she was reading.

She replied "Well, the type of books I read are either called urban fiction, street lit, or hip-hop fiction. They're mostly written by people who've come from the 'hood. I like 'em because I can relate to a lot of 'em, so I haven't been able to stay out of the bookstore. Anyway, the book I'm reading now is called *Ghetto Diva* by Brandy. She's one of the best. I like her not only because she's from LA, but because I can relate to her and what she write about."

I nodded. This was my first time hearing of street lit. I was more into authors like Toni Morrison, James Baldwin, Terry McMillan, Ralph Ellison, and Walter Mosley. I asked, "So where can I find these type of books?"

"Wherever books are sold. You could even find these type of books on the New York Times bestseller's list. Anyway, I got two more pages left with this book, I'll let you borrow it at the end of lunch to see if you like it or not. But when you get finished, I want my book back. I keep all my books."

Girl, I Had Enough!

After lunch, Monica handed me Ghetto Diva and went to her fifth period class. I didn't have a fifth or sixth period class, so I sat reading *Ghetto Diva*. I found the book to be exciting and a page turner. I loved the raw grammar and sexy gangster situations in the book. The book was well-written with salacious content and lots of drama. The storyline was about a sister who was in a very abusive relationship with the father of her two children. The one time she stood up for herself, the system end up taking her children and placing them in the custody of the father. *Ghetto Diva*, as the sister call herself, ended up doing everything in her power to get her kids back, even frame the father of her children.

After reading *Ghetto Diva* in one sit down, the thought of helping Calvin popped fully into my head. I sat minutes on the hour scheming on how I could turn Calvin's situation around. Then, it all came to me. "What goes around comes around," I told myself with a snide grin spread across my face. "Just like *Ghetto Diva* framed her baby daddy and you framed Calvin, I'ma frame you."

I was plotting evil, and my first plan of operation was to find out as much about Alice's boyfriend as I could. Joy supplied me with all the information I needed. Tyree, also known as Tyson, was a Crip. He had spent most of his life behind bars for various crimes, such as robbery, possession with intent to sell, and assault. And he was a prime candidate for the "HE AIN'T SHIT!" award. Joy had even told me he gawked her up and down lustfully everyday, so I knew what I had to do. I had to dress like a whore. I had on a mini-skirt with no drawls underneath, a halter top with no bra so my perky breasts and nipples could stand out. I got my weave tightened to perfection. I tucked a small handgun into my purse just in case I had to save my son. I didn't want to involve Charles, but he wouldn't let me go alone or with anyone else. He felt it was only right to help his father.

"Okay, Charles, here we go," I said, trembling at the lips and shaking like a paranoid crack addict. "You know the plan. Joy gave you the keys to the back door, so make sure your tall butt stays low. Move swift like a marine, stash the whole bag of drugs and guns in their closet, and get the hell out. You understand?" Charles nodded. "Yes." I could tell this was an adventure to him. He was rubbing his Nike gloves together and blowing into them. I was so scared, I was on the verge of calling the mission off. Then, Alice drove by. It looked like she was going off on Joy. Joy was up her rear, in the backseat, with her face pressed against the window looking like she was a lost puppy. The twins were next to her in the rear. Bill was in the passenger seat playing Game Boy.

Joy furrowed her brows as they passed. This gave me the strength to go on with the mission. I didn't want to let her down; she was willing to do anything in her power to keep her father from going to prison. I actually felt bad for her. She felt it was her fault Calvin was in the situation he was in, which was not true.

After Alice turned the corner, Charles and I leapt from the car. I let him get a slight lead in front of me. My son carried himself and the duffle bag swiftly through the wind. His lanky legs took giant steps. He was speed walking. I wanted to tell him to slow down, but before I could say anything, he had already turned into his father's yard headed for the back door. I had to put my fears to the side and put pep in my step.

I made it to the front door and pounded on it. I knew Tyson was in the house somewhere. Joy had called and confirmed it before they left. "Who is it?" a deep voice asked.

I replied, "Brandy." That was the first name to pop into my head. My nipples were bulging through the halter top fully erect.

Tyson opened the wooden door and screwed his face. "Who?"

"Brandy," I said in a sexy voice.

When he spotted me through the screen door, his whole demeanor changed. He had a wifebeater on and was holding his daughter in his arms. He opened the screen door invitingly. His well-defined biceps were evidence of the many years he spent incarcerated. I started tapping my foot nervously. I knew I had to keep him occupied for at least, three to five minutes, and by the way he was gawking me, I knew that wasn't

Girl, I Had Enough!

going to be hard. I was just hoping he didn't try to pull me in the house or anything of that nature. He was already eye-raping me. He was so lustfully staring, he didn't even ask who I was looking for.

I said. "Hi! Is Joy home?"

"Who?" he asked as if he was deaf. He was too busy staring at my nipples to grasp what I had asked him.

"Joy," I said, tooting my lips up and folding my arms across my chest, letting him know I knew what he was staring at.

He chuckled, dug in his pocket, and pulled out a pack of Newports. He said, "No. Joy's not here." The newborn was still in his arms as he took a cancer stick out of the pack with his lips. It hung from the corner of his mouth.

I decided to change the subject. I figured Charles had probably just entered the house, so I had to hold Tyson hostage another two or three minutes. "Well, do you know what time she'll be back?"

"Naw," he said bluntly.

I removed my arms from my chest to gain his attention. "Well, if you don't mind me asking, may I ask who are you? Because this is my first time seeing you. You ain't her fine-ass uncle she always talk about, are you?"

Tyson smiled, showing his tobacco-stained teeth. I furrowed my brows like "Ugh!" I couldn't see what Alice found attractive in him. I figured where he lacked in looks, he made up for elsewhere. I took it that he was working with a monster penis, because Calvin was well-hung and self-reliant. So I figured he had to been working with at least ten inches of steel.

He said, "Little Momma, I'm whoever you want me to be."

Out the corner of my eyes, I saw Charles exiting the yard. Yes, I thought. Perfect timing, baby. I folded my arms across my chest again and told Tyson, "Well, tell Joy I came by. Also, it's not good to smoke in front of your newborn child."

Terry Wroten

I turned on my heels and headed down the porch and out the yard, holding my skirt down so my backside wouldn't show. I looked over my shoulder as I exited the yard and finger-waved. Tyson was still gawking. I shook my head. Fuckin' pervert, I thought.

I made it to the car, smiling from ear to ear. Charles was smiling just the same. I gave him a high five as I entered the car. "Did we pull that off or what?" I asked.

"As easy as one, two, three," Charles said excitedly.

"Well, give me a hug, because I was scared shitless until you motivated me with your 'lets get it' attitude. Anyhow, we got a few hours before court is over, so that gives me enough time to go change these ho'ish clothes."

Charles nodded. "Well, have you made up your mind what you are going to say when you call 911?"

I smiled. A devilish grin stretched across my face. "Sure have."

"We going to be sitting right here when they pull up, and as soon as they do, I'm dialing 911. '911, what's your emergency?' Hello! This is an anonymous caller. I'd like to report Alice Williams and her live-in boyfriend of 4342 South San Pedro. They're selling crack cocaine and guns out of their house with five different minors living in there. You need to send a couple units over there, because just a little while ago, a drug deal went bad, guns were drawn, and the buyer said he'll be back. There's kids in the house and I fear for their lives. Thank You. Have a nice day."

I had everything under control. The hard part was done. Charles slapped five again. "Ma, I'm glad you and my dad are getting along and making things easier on me. It feels good to have both my parents on good terms."

I ran my hand across his chin. "This should teach you something. When a woman's fed up, all hell break loose and it's nothing you could do about it. R. Kelly said it best."

ALICE

39

Your honor, now on the child support issue, we've already informed the courts that Mrs. Williams is a swindler and a very larcenous woman. We recently discovered some new information that we'd like to submit to you before you make your findings."

I was in court listening to this bitch Shalon run her mouth about this, about that, and a lot of other shit that had nothing to her or nothing to do with the case. I was hotter than fish grease. I sat tapping my foot impatiently with my arms folded across my chest. I was mad at myself for being cheap and not hiring a lawyer, and I was fuming because the presiding judge wasn't trying to hear anything I had to say. The funny thing is, she was a middle-aged black woman who I felt would be fair and stand up for sistahood, but I was wrong!

At one point, she asked to hear from just the husband and wife. Shalon took a seat and Calvin stood up. She said, "Mr. Williams, I'd like to hear from you first."

Calvin got right to talking. He had this fake innocent posture about himself that made me grunt, "Humph!" I just stood with my arms folded across my chest and my lips tooted. I couldn't wait to hear what he had to say.

"Well, your honor, I met Mrs. Williams approximately nineteen years ago at a Lakers game. I found her to be a very comely woman.

Terry Wroten

We began to date, and even though I was driving to Watts, The Projects, to pick her up every day, I found her character to be drama-free. Well, that's what I thought. After two years of dating and messing around, Alice conceived our first child. I was the proudest father in the world. Then, within a year, Alice was pregnant again with our second child. Now, 'bout time her third pregnancy came around, I'd made a big mistake. Well, it wasn't a mistake, because I love my son, Charles, but I cheated on Alice with a teacher I met named Charlene Hunt. Alice and I would eventually split up over this . . ."

"No. Tell the truth," I chimed in. "She called the house. I answered the phone. She asked was I your wife. I said 'yes'. She told me you lied to her and told her you were single with no kids. Then, she told me she was pregnant. And the sad part about it is, you didn't deny it like most dogs will do . . ."

"Okay Mrs. Williams, that's enough. Let me hear from your husband first, then you can speak your piece."

I hated the whole court process. I nodded briskly to the judge and Calvin continued.

"Well, as she just said, I didn't deny anything. And reason being, I knew I was wrong. We split up for a year and some change, but what she don't know and didn't know I found out, she was cheating on me before she even found out about Charlene. And the worst thing is, I have a porno of her in the projects giving sexual favors to a group of men. However, I never said nothing…"

"Your Honor, that's a lie," I intervened.

"I got the tape right here, if the court want to see it."

Calvin raised his hand showing a videotape. My heart dropped. I don't know how he came up with that tape, but I knew I did do a porno for Joe. I got paid $1,000, but it wasn't worth the shame I felt. I was hoping like hell the judge didn't play the tape.

"Ah, Mr. Williams, that's okay. The court will take your word on this one. Continue."

Girl, I Had Enough!

"Well, I like I was saying, Alice didn't know any of this information, and I never brought it up, because I feel two wrongs don't make a right. Plus, we had three beautiful children that needed both their parents. So we ended up getting back together, but we have never been the same. She's used my one wrong to cheat with over twenty different men, then throw it in my face when I catch her. She's made my life a living hell for the last fourteen years, even burnt down our first house while I was asleep. She tried to kill me because I wouldn't get up and hear what she had to say, but I didn't press charges. I just got as far away from her as I could. Then, most recently, she filed some fictitious attempted murder charge on me. The police come kicking in my girlfriend's door like they were looking for a serial rapist or killer, and embarrassed my girlfriend, who happens to be a doctor and lives in a predominately all white neighborhood."

I stood listening to Calvin, tapping my foot impatiently. I wanted to interrupt him so bad, but I didn't want to get on the judge's bad side. I held my tongue and stared at him. I gave him and everyone else in the court room the evil eye, especially that fat-bubble-gut-bitch Lola. She sat behind him with one thigh over the other, looking like an elephant.

"Then, the papers and letters my lawyer will submit to you will show you what kind of woman Alice really is. And to add fuel to the fire, she has an ex-convict living in my house with my children and they are selling drugs, guns, and doing all kinds of illegal activities…"

"That's a lie, Your Honor," I chimed, in frowning. "That's a lie, and Calvin knows it. He's a habitual liar. He - "

"Okay. Mrs. Williams, it's still not your turn."

The judge did not want to hear my side of the story for nothing in the world. I decided to take a seat and let Calvin say what he had to say. When it was my turn, I got up and said what I had to say. To sum everything up, I simply told the judge that Calvin wasn't shit! He was a liar! A cheater! Deceiver! And heartbreaker!

231

Terry Wroten

After I spoke my peace, Shalon jumped up. "Your Honor, I have before me some papers and documents that I'd like to submit from a man named Byron Woods."

My heart dropped. I knew what was coming next. I wondered how in the hell they found out about Byron? The only person that knew I was working Byron was me. I guess what you do in the dark always come to the light, huh?

"Byron Woods is an ex-lover of Mrs. Williams, who she has been conning and deceitfully misleading to extort money from. She called my client a liar, cheater, deceiver, and heartbreaker. Well, I find it interesting that these papers and documents that I'm holding before you will only prove that Mrs. Williams is all of the above characteristics and is once again trying her best to deceive someone. And that someone just so happens to be you."

Shalon handed the bailiff the papers. The bailiff handed them to the judge. I sat there anticipating defeat, but to my luck, the judge said, "Let's go to recess while I go over these papers." She banged her gavel, and I was out the door with the kids right behind me.

CHARLENE

40

G irl, she just stormed out of the courtroom mad," Lola informed. "Shalon just submitted the papers Byron faxed Calvin to the judge, and the judge called for a two-day recess. I guess Alice sees her plan crumbling, so she's very upset. I take it she'll be pulling up to her house within no time, so I'm just calling to give you the heads up."

I hung up with Lola and cracked a one-sided smile. I looked over to Charles and told him, "They're on their way".

A snide grin stretched across his face. "'Bout time," he hissed.

We waited a good thirty minutes after receiving the call from Lola before Alice pulled up. You could tell she was hotter than fish grease and taking it all out on Joy. Joy looked like a lost cause. She looked my way as she exited the car, and I said, "Hold strong, it won't be long."

It seemed like Joy was prisoner of war. For lack of definition, she was! She was caught up in the middle of her parents' bullshit and you could just see all the wear and tear it was having on her.

As soon as they entered the house, I dialed 911. "911, what's your emergency?"

"Hello, this is anonymous caller . . ."

I played my role to the fullest. I told the dispatcher that the house was supposed to be getting shot up over a drug deal gone bad, and that the kids living in the house were in danger. I even told the woman where

Terry Wroten

Charles stashed the duffle bag of guns and drugs. Before I knew it, police was everywhere. Even a helicopter hovered above. Law enforcement ran into Alice's house like dogs to a hot bitch.

Charles and I sat and watched as LAPD brought Tyson and Alice out of the house in handcuffs. Alice was kicking and screaming. You could tell she was having a bad day. And how she was cursing out Tyson, I just knew she figured the duffle bag was his. I heard some of her raving. She said, "Muhfucka, no wonder why you wanted me to leave so fast earlier. I got kids. You betta take yo' own beef."

Tyson frowned, "Bitch, you got me fucked up! That ain't my shit. This ain't my house. I don't live here."

Charles smiled. "Yes!" He kissed me on the cheek. "Ma, we did it. Now, let's call my dad to come get my brother and sisters."

I called Calvin and gave him the news. His only reply was, "Damn, girl, I told you, you didn't have to go out your way to save me. But shit, when a woman's fed up, it ain't nothing you can do about it, huh?"

I laughed. "Nope. Anyway, come get my son's brother and sisters before I really get fed up."

I hung up feeling like a new woman. Payback's a mutha . . .

ZENA

41

I'd been out shopping all day. Rasheed has been staying with his parents on and off for the last five months. The only time he came home was to change his clothes or to see his daughter. He told me he wasn't coming back home until I stop nagging him, but I wasn't stupid. He was cheating on me, and I just knew it. My heart was telling me. I had all the clues, I just couldn't prove it.

However, it was a week before Maryam's third birthday. I had borrowed Rasheed's truck to go get all the stuff for her party. We swapped vehicles for the whole week. Rasheed's only concern was for me to take his truck to the car wash. I did just that after two days of having the truck.

As I sat reading an Essence magazine, one of the guys who was cleaning the truck walked up to me and asked, "Is dis yours?" He was a small Mexican man with a deep accent. He said, "I find on de ground, but I think it falla out your truck when I clean inside."

I grabbed the book from the man and read the cover: *Freaky Extortions: When Nature Calls.* By Tiffany Childs, aka NaughtyGirl69.

"Humph!" I smirked opening the book.

Inside, the cover page read:

Terry Wroten

Dear Rasheed,

I hope you enjoy. I know you're a busy man, so if you can't read the whole book, at least read chapter ten and tell me what you think and how you feel? My number (909) 555-4248.

Tiffany Childs even signed the book with a heart and happy face. I immediately told the small Mexican man that the book belonged to me. I then, turned to chapter ten. I was curious to know what was so important about chapter ten that she wanted him to read so bad.

Chapter Ten was called "DickGameProper". That set off a five-fire alarm in my head. I was onto something. DickGameProper was the name Rasheed called himself on Myspace. I immediately started reading word for word. 'Bout the time I got done with chapter ten, I had all the answers I needed. That no good muhfucka! Rasheed was cheating on me. My mind started racing. I hurriedly hopped in Rasheed's truck headed home to get my gun.

"His dog-ass gon' pay!"

Tears rushed to my eyes and streamed down my face. I was hurt and I was tired. I was exhausted. Rah had played me too thin this time. He'd fucked the bitch in the ass, in the rain, and sucked her pussy. And probably came home and kissed me. My husband had committed the ultimate betrayal, not once, but twice!

I tried to laugh the pain off by saying, "It's okay. Every dog has his day." But that didn't work. I got stabbed in the heart one too many times, and this time the wound wouldn't stop bleeding. It felt like I was dying a slow death.

I called Rasheed before I made it home. I was crying nonstop and wouldn't tell him the reason. I just told him it was an emergency. He hopped in my car and made it home before me.

When I arrived home I pulled into the driveway and played it off good. I didn't tell him the obvious, I just sobbed and told him, "I was out shopping and something bad happened." I didn't tell him what, because I needed to buy enough time to get into the house and grabbed

Girl, I Had Enough!

my gun.

Rasheed followed me into the house, asking, "What's wrong? I ignored him. He grabbed me by the arms and turned me to him. He sternly said, "Zena, Goddamnit, tell me what's wrong!"

I had one grocery bag in my hand that concealed the book. The evidence, as I called it. I wanted to throw the bag at him and tell him to open it. However, I about-faced and kept walking in the room.

As soon as I entered the room, I went straight to my Coach bag. Then, it registered in Rasheed's head what I was doing. His eyes widened and he seethed, "Zena, whatta hell-fuck you doin'?"

I retrieved my .50 cal and threw the grocery bag at Rah. The book fell out, and he knew he was busted. To my surprise, the nigga didn't try to deny it. He turned on his heels and tried to run for dear life.

Like a motion picture in slow motion, I aimed and watched as sparks fired from out of my gun and bullets ripped into Rasheed's back. Out of fear and adrenaline rush, the slugs didn't slow him down. He raced out of the house and across the street.

I raced right behind his firing.

Boom, boom, boom, boom, boom, boom!

I fired all six rounds from the revolver, hitting Rah with each slug, but he was trying his damndest to escape death. He stayed on his feet and collapsed at the front door of Jennifer's house.

Jennifer came running out of her house. "Ooh! Rasheed, what happened?"

Jennifer had tears in her eyes. This verified my suspicion about them fucking each other. I pointed my gun at Jennifer and pulled the trigger.

Click!

Click!

I ran out of ammunition. I snapped, "You white bitch, I knew you were fuckin' my husband! You gon' get yours too."

I turned back toward the house and ran to retrieve my .9mm. I was irritated with myself for not grabbing my gun that held the most bullets.

Terry Wroten

. After I grabbed my .9mm from underneath my mattress, I ran back outside. But as soon as I exited the house, a police squad car was bending the corner onto the block. I ran back into the house, locked the door, and started contemplating suicide. I didn't know if I killed Rah or not, but I heard sirens roaring. I didn't want to live any longer. I loved Rasheed, but why did he have to cheat on me?

I looked down the barrel of my gun. My trigger finger was itching. I was inches away from taking my own life. Then, I looked around my house and spotted my family portrait on the wall. I looked at Maryam, then at Calvin. I looked at them for five minutes straight, then dropped my gun. I ran over to my house phone and called Jada. She had Maryam at her house. I told Jada I shot Calvin and that the police were outside of my house.

She asked, "Did you kill him?"

I told her, "I don't know."

She let out a deep breath. "Okay. Stay where you are. I was chillin' with my little friend TLW, but we on our way."

I hung up with Jada, then called Poppa. I didn't know what to tell him when he answered, I just sobbed, "Poppa, I just shot my husband."

Poppa replied. "Damn! I done told that boy."

He sounded like he had predicted the future. He didn't even sound mad that I'd shot his own son. He asked, "Is he still alive?"

I told him," I don't know." He ended up telling me to stay put until he got to the house, but it was too late. LAPD was already knocking down the door . . .

TREY
42

J ust when I thought it couldn't get any worse, I come home to no home. Sheila had robbed me dry. She even took Candy with her. The funny thing is, she played her cards perfectly. She had KC move to Atlanta first. A month later, she moved and took everything! A couple weeks after she left, Candy handed me a big yellow envelope and told me she'd be right back. That was the last time I had seen her.

Inside the envelope was a videotape. Since I had nowhere to stay, I went to the club to watch it. Unbelievably, there it was, Sheila, KC, and Candy ass-naked getting their freak on.

I couldn't do nothing but laugh to myself, because I knew I got what I deserved. At the end of the porno, in BIG BOLD letters, it read:

WHEN A WOMAN'S FED UP . . . BABY, IT AIN'T NOTHING YOU COULD DO ABOUT IT!!! HAVE A NICE AND HAPPY 'BROKE' LIFE . . .

I laughed out loud while sipping on some Jack Daniels. I thought about my brothers. Calvin, was completing a one-year bid. Byrd got the attempted murder stopped, but Calvin pleaded no contest for punching that cop in the face. Lola had his daughter the day before he had to turn himself in. She named her Alexia-Alexis Angel Williams, because it turns out the twins weren't his or Byron's. But being the man Calvin is, they're still part of the family and still his daughters. Since Alice receved three-years for the guns and drugs found in her house, Poppa has custody of the kids until Calvin's release. Alice could have gotten more time than she got, but she turned state's evidence on Tyson. She pointed him out in front of a grand jury and lied. She blamed him for the guns and drugs being in her house. She told the jury that he wasn't worth shit and she was fed up with his shit. Hand over fist, Tyson received a life sentence. The sad part is, through all the bullshit my niece, Joy, ended up pregnant. Come to find out, she don't know who the baby father is. CJ and Trevon are the only two doing good. They're blowing up in the music industry. They even have a song on the Billboard 100 called "Get Better, Uncle Rah".

Zena shot Rasheed six times in the back. He's been in the hospital for the last nine months. She was in jail standing trail, but Poppa was trying to get her out. He had Byrd on the case. Jada had custody of Maryam. Word has it that she's sleeping with a young Crip turned book writer and he was brainstorming a book called *When A Woman's Fed Up*.

"Humph!" I chuckled out loud. I was now tipsy, thinking about how everything had played out for me and my brothers. I told myself, "Shit, if that nigga want a story, I got one for him. Shit, how bad I need the money, nigga, where you at . . ."

Knock!

Knock!

My thought were derailed when Fat Pat came knocking on my office door. I buzzed him in. He walked in saying, "What it do, boss? What we got going for these ho's? Because you know we got Ayana, Diamond, and Miss New Booty down for whatever like four flat tires . . ."

I cracked a one-sided smile and shook my head. Life is a bitch. I played with pussy and got fucked, but Sheila and KC played with my dick so I get the last nut!

I laughed to myself, "HA!"

"LAUGH NOW, CRY LATER, B-I-T-C-H-E-S . . ."

Acknowledgements

To the mother of my child, Lureon Jackson, for forever putting up with my unpredictable self. To my many aunties Toni, Raquel, Dee, Niece, & Samantha. My authors: Brandy Lerue, Erica Renee, Bnote, Cal Blue, and Joel Arnold. My WCAM (WESTCOAST AUTHOR MOVEMENT) family: Author Mimi Renee, Raynesha Pittman, Kelly Wiley, Cha'bella Don, MG Hardie, Rickey Teems II, N.S Real Lit.

To all my readers and supporters:

Tikki, Neto, TC, Little Man, Kboy, Second II None MC, Fudgy-Fudge, Lil Stone, CT, D-Mac, G-Eyes 1-4, Yung Dopey, D-Man, Spider3, Anthony "HP" Ennis, Redd, JG, T-Hottie, Pill, Tay-Tay (thumbs up!), Jan Weldon-Vietch, Deborah Cardona aka Sexy, Kwan, June Miller, Erick Gray, Treasure Blue, Zeus BigHap Villegas, Ray Porter, Leatha Writes, Jina Love, Ra shawn Da-Professor Chisolm, Jennifer Williams, Devon Booker, Raenisha Smith, Destiny Smith, the ladies of ARC Book Club Inc(English Rules, Shai, Sistar Tea, & Locksie), Mollie Jones, Wanda Jones, Tragedy Dark, Elois Thames, Frann Bynes, Shondayah Pegram, Yolanda Black, Ieasha Wilson, Black Angel LA Smith, Cotrena Taylor, Shoney K Upcoming Actress, Britt Roach, Lady Spider (my sister who love to hate me), Tasha Nairn, Shanika Martin, Sharon Gxngstx, Tammy Kidd-Julien, Chicc Thomas, Dramenia Williams, Chuncky Dopeness, Tasha Rubio, Angela Bowman, Carol Hammond, Felita Hammond, Andre Hammond, Ambrose Beard, Tra Curry, L Boog, Rahiem Wingate, Yolanda Shavette, Naomi B. Johnson, Tureko Thomas, BeNita Grant, Latosha Holmes, Chanel Johnson(Mama),Tashie Taylor, Whitey(Scrap Mama), Tee-Tee Gatlin, SpySee Hott & the whole High Desert Finest SC, Kayla Scurlock, Byte Syze, Anjela Day, Priccilla Portillo, Brandance Nathan-Marsh, Genessa & Chris Martin, the ladies and gents of BFSB Book Club (Carla Towns, Sandy Barrett Sims, Tonikia Trotter, Lanesha Nene Marie Allen, Jennifer Martin, Zaneta Powell, Gabrielle GotemHatin Dotson,

Shantelle Brown, Twana Spencer, Madonna Awotwi), Twilla Sanders, Sabrina Bennett, Candise Isblessed, Mac Blu, Marissa Palmer, Keioka Harris, Autumn Wright, Moma Boo Boo, Romonica Bass, Crystal Brown, Lakeisha Allen, Meka Stokes, Nadine Hill, Lisa Carlos, Christine Paul, Sharira Thomas, Kenya Ikeda Moses, RIM BOOK CLUB (special shout to Minah Diggs), all the bike clubs and social clubs that support me, all my Blood relatives yall know who yall are, and last but not least to all my niggaz locked behind them walls keep your head up, come home and keep God first... TLW

Made in the USA
San Bernardino, CA
17 August 2014